GW01099931

Favourite Tales from Hans Christian Andersen

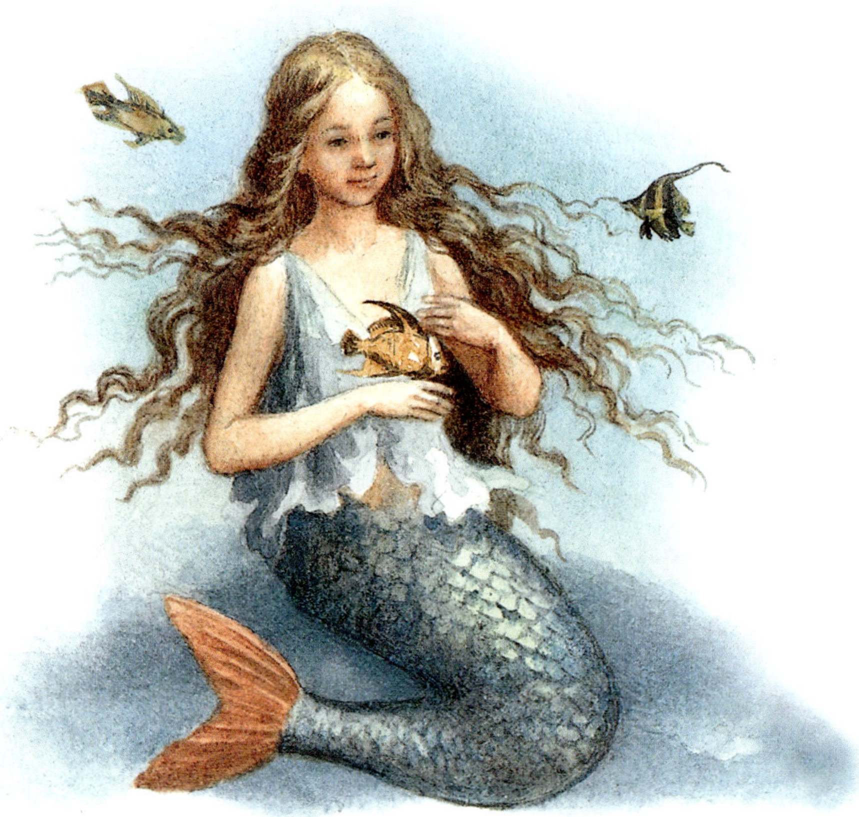

Favourite Tales from Hans Christian Andersen

Illustrated by Anastasiya Archipova

Floris Books

This edition published in 2001 by Floris Books
15 Harrison Gardens, Edinburgh
Reprinted in 2006

© 1999 Esslinger Verlag J. F. Schreiber GmbH, Esslingen Germany
English version © 2001 Floris Books
British Library CIP Data available
ISBN 0-86315-347-X
Printed in Spain

Contents

The Swineherd	7
The Princess and the Pea	27
The Snow Queen	35
The Emperor's New Suit	59
The Brave Tin Soldier	81
The Little Match-Seller	99
The Little Mermaid	121
The Fir Tree	165
The Storyteller: Hans Christian Andersen	190

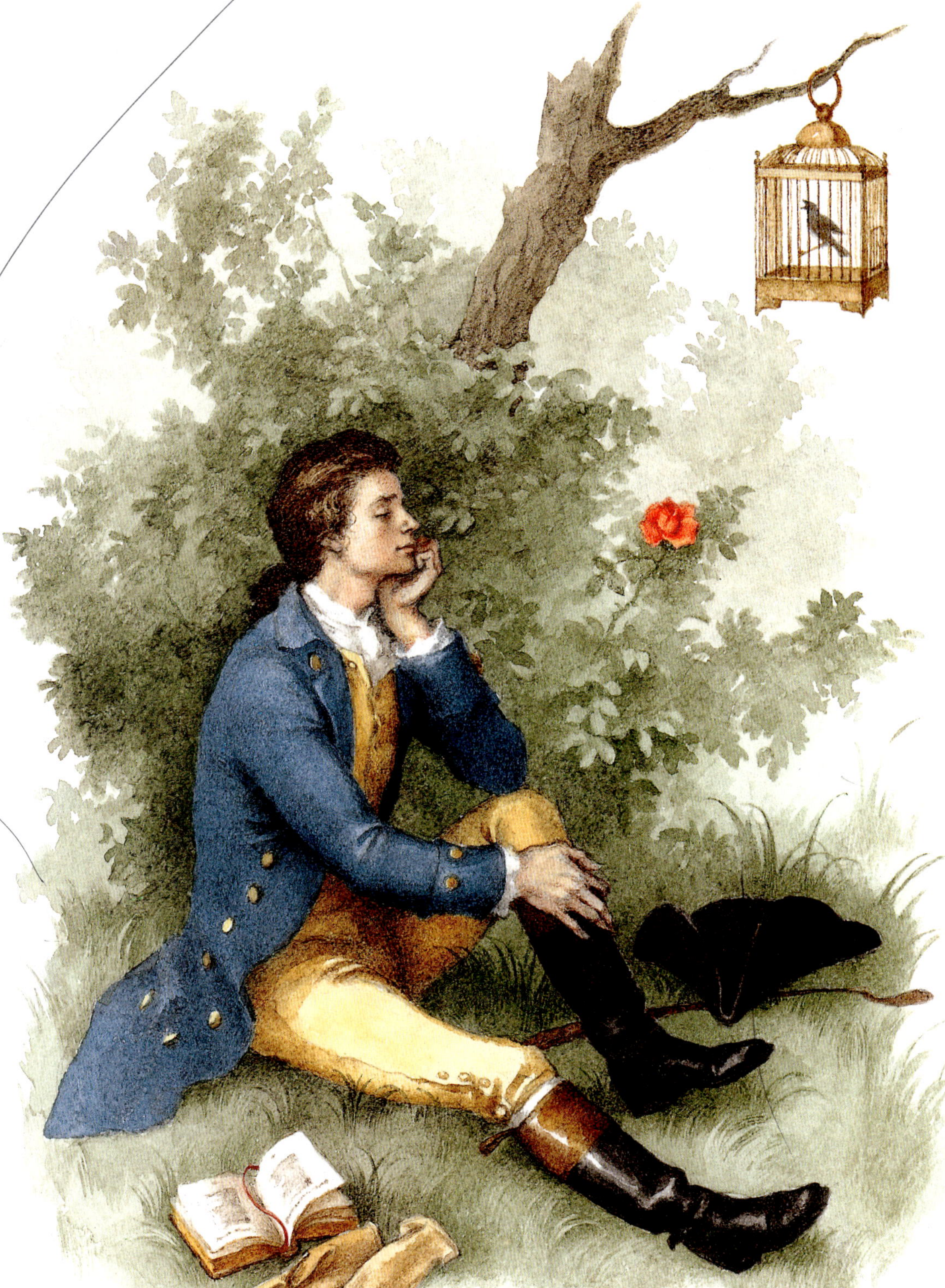

The Swineherd

ONCE upon a time there was a poor prince. He had a kingdom which was rather small, but, small or not, it was large enough to marry on, and marry he would.

Now, it was really rather forward of him, daring to say to the emperor's daughter: "Will you have me?" But he did dare, for his name was famous everywhere. There were hundreds of princesses who would have said "Yes" and been glad of him. But do you think she did? Well now, just listen.

Growing on the grave of the prince's father was a rose-tree — such a lovely rose-tree! It flowered only once every five years, and even then it only had one bloom; but this rose was so sweet that to smell it made you forget all your troubles and worries. And then he had a nightingale, which could sing as though every lovely melody sat in its little throat.

The prince decided that the rose and the nightingale were for the princess; and so they were both placed in big silver caskets and sent to her.

The emperor had them carried before him into the great hall where the princess was playing hunt the thimble with her maids of honour — they never did anything else. And when she saw the big caskets with the presents inside, she clapped her hands for joy.

"I do hope it's a little kitten!" she said. But then out came the beautiful rose.

"Oh, isn't it pretty!" cried all the maids of honour.

"It's more than pretty," said the emperor; "it's really nice!"

But then the princess felt it, and she could have cried.

"Ugh, daddy!" she cried. "It isn't an imitation one: it's real!"

"Ugh!" cried all the maids of honour. "It's a real one!"

"Now, let's see what's in the other casket before we start getting upset!" suggested the emperor. And then out came the nightingale; and sang so beautifully that for the moment nobody could find any fault with it.

"*Superbe! Charmant!*" cried all the maids of honour; because they all spoke French, the one worse than the other.

"How the bird reminds me of the late lamented empress's musical-box!" said an old courtier. "Why yes, it's exactly the same tone, the same expression!"
"Yes, it is!" said the emperor; and he cried like a child.

"I don't believe that's a real one!" said the princess.

"Oh yes, that's a real bird!" said the men who had brought it.

"Then away with the creature!" said the princess. So the maids opened the window and let the bird fly off. And the princess wouldn't hear of allowing the prince in.

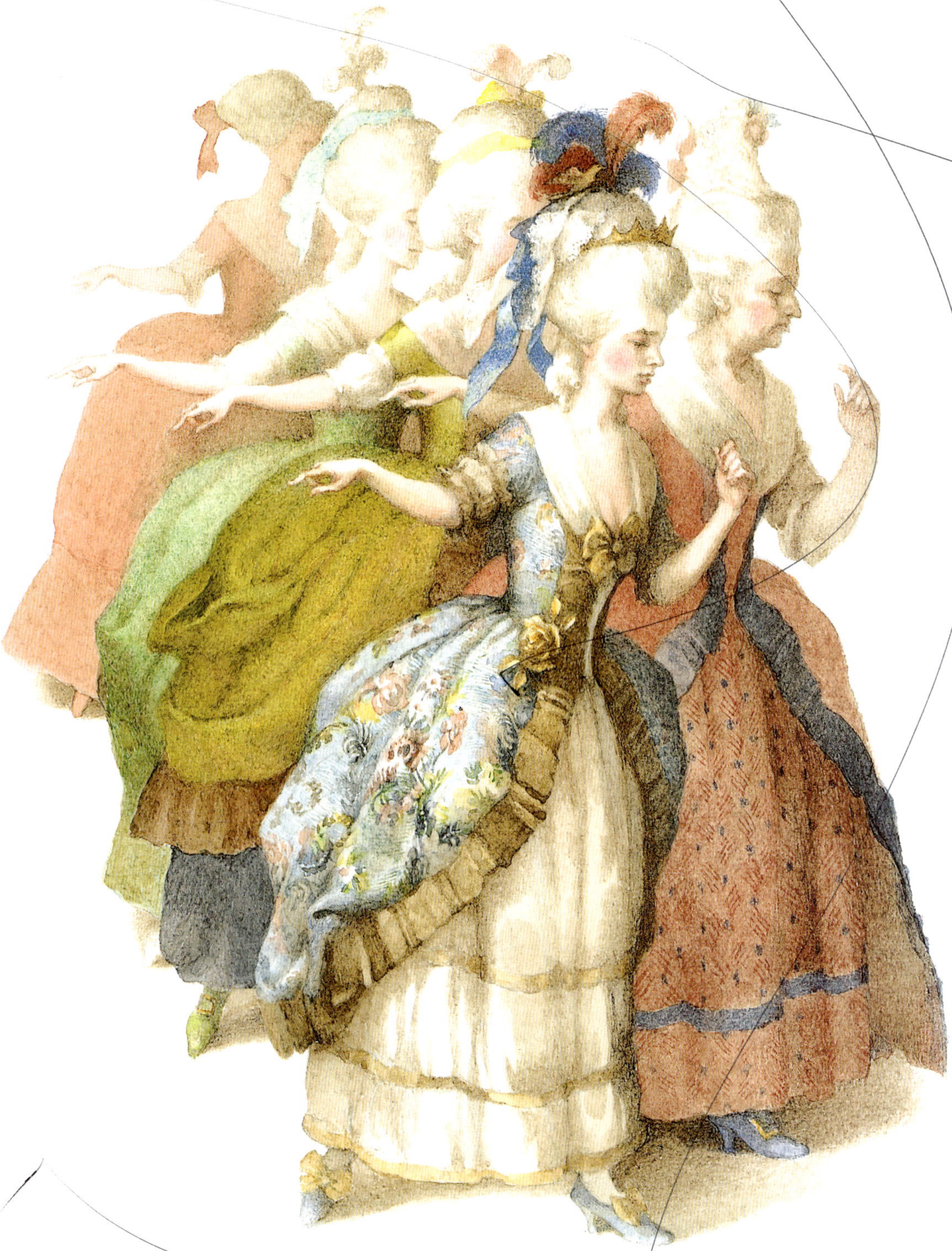

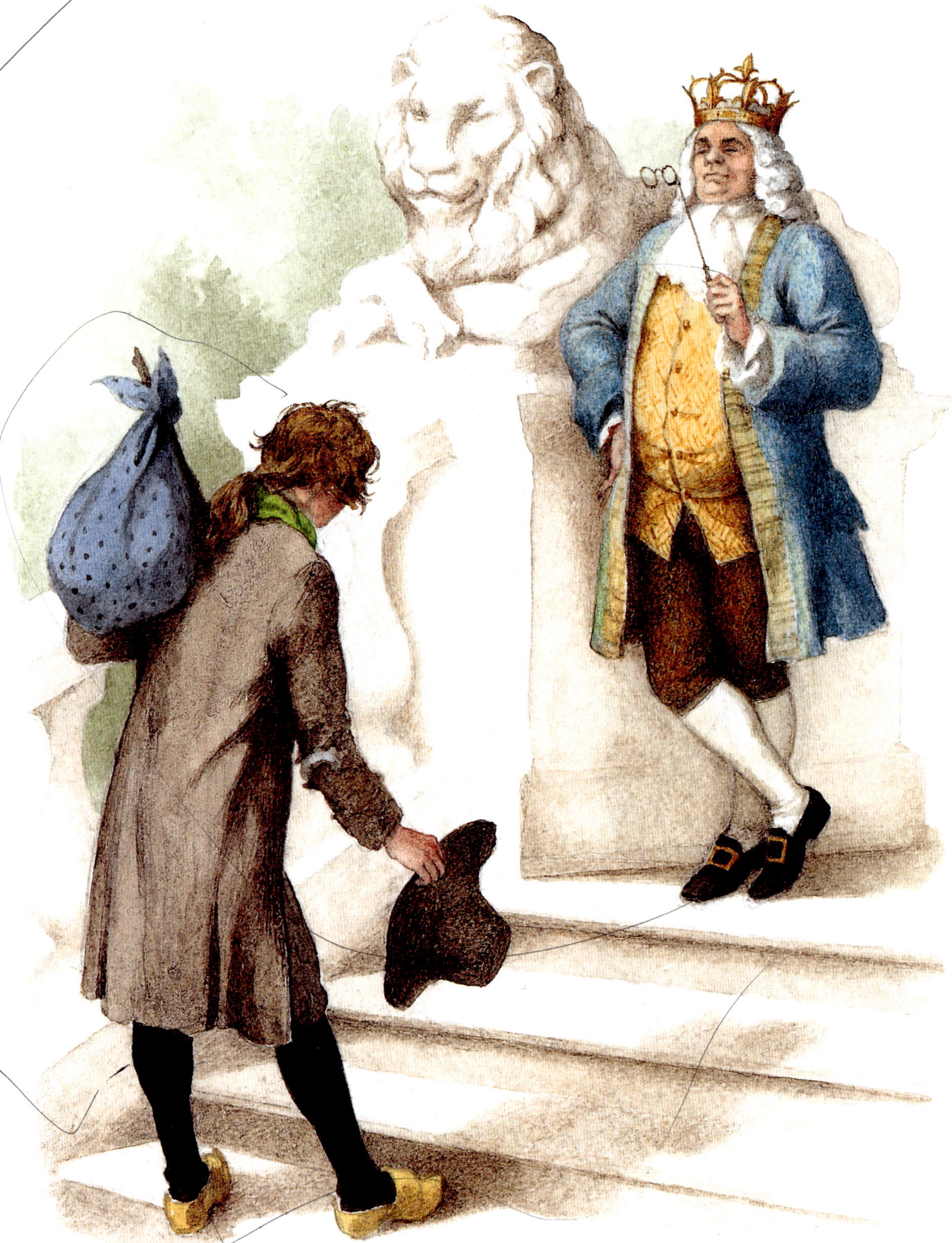

But the prince wasn't to be put off like that. He smeared his face black and brown, pulled his cap down over his eyes, and knocked at the gate.

"Good morning, emperor!" he said. "Have you a job for me at the palace?"

"Well, we get so many coming and asking for jobs!" said the emperor. "But let me see — I could do with somebody to look after the pigs! We've got so many of them."

And so the prince was taken on as Imperial Swineherd. He was given a wretched little room down by the pigsty, and there he had to stay. But he sat working away all day long, and by evening he had made a nice little cooking-pot. All round it there were little bells, and as soon as the pot started to boil they would tinkle away so prettily, playing the old tune of:

> Ah, my darling Augustine,
> Everything's lost, lost, lost!

But the oddest thing of all was that if you held your finger in the steam which came from the pot, you could immediately smell what was being cooked in every oven in the town. Well now, that was a different thing altogether from a rose.

Now, the princess was walking past with all her maids of honour, and when she heard the tune she stood still and looked very pleased, because she too could play "Ah, my darling Augustine." It was the only tune she could play, but then she played it with one finger.

"Why, that's the tune I know!" she said. "Then he must be a well-bred swineherd. I say! Go in and ask him the price of that instrument!"

And so one of the maids of honour had to run in and ask. But she put clogs on first.

"What will you take for that pot?" asked the maid of honour.
"Ten kisses from the princess!" answered the swineherd.
"Good gracious me!" said the maid of honour.
"Nothing else will do!" said the swineherd.
"Well, what's he say?" asked the princess.
"I really can't tell you!" said the lady. "It's so shocking!"
"Then whisper it to me!" And so she whispered it.
"How very rude he is!" said the princess, walking away at once.

But she hadn't gone far when the bells began tinkling again.

"Look here!" said the princess. "Ask him if he'll take ten kisses from my maids of honour!"

"No, thanks!" said the swineherd. "Ten kisses from the princess, or I stick to my pot!"

"How very tiresome!" said the princess. "But then you must all of you stand round me, so nobody sees!"

So the maids of honour all stood round, spreading out their dresses; and the swineherd got his ten kisses, and she her pot. And then they did have fun! All that evening and next day the pot was kept on the boil. There wasn't an oven in the town but they knew what was being cooked there, from the chamberlain's to the cobbler's. They all clapped their hands in delight.

"We know who's having soup and pancakes! We know who's having roast and rice pudding! How interesting it all is!"

"Most interesting!" said the lady stewardess.

"Yes, but no telling, mind!" said the princess. "Because I'm the emperor's daughter!"

"We'd never dream of telling!" they all said.

The swineherd — that is to say, the prince, but of course they had no idea that he wasn't a real swineherd — the swineherd never missed a day without doing something. And now he made a rattle. When he swung it round, it played all the waltzes, jigs, and polkas that had ever been known.

"Oh, isn't it *superbe!*" cried the princess, as she was passing. "I never heard such a lovely composition! Look here, go and ask him the price of that instrument! But there'll be no kissing!"

"He wants a hundred kisses from your royal highness!" said the maid of honour who had been to ask.

"The fellow must be mad!" said the princess, and she walked off. But she had not gone very far when she stopped. "We must encourage the arts!" she said. "And I'm the emperor's daughter! Tell him he shall have ten kisses, the same as yesterday. The rest he can take from my maids of honour!"

"Oh, but we wouldn't like him to!" said the maids of honour.

"Nonsense!" said the princess. "If I can kiss him, so can you!"

And so the maid of honour had to go in again.

"A hundred kisses from the princess," he said; "or we both keep what we've got!"

"Stand round!" the princess said. And so all the maids of honour stood round, and he began his kisses.

"What on earth is all that commotion down by the pigsty?" said the emperor, who had stepped out on to the balcony; and he rubbed his eyes and put on his spectacles. "If it isn't the maids of honour up to their tricks! I'll have to see to them!" And he pulled his slippers up behind, and how he hurried!

Once down in the courtyard, he crept along very quietly; and the maids of honour were so busy counting the kisses to see that all was fair, and that the swineherd didn't get too many nor too few, that none of them noticed the emperor.

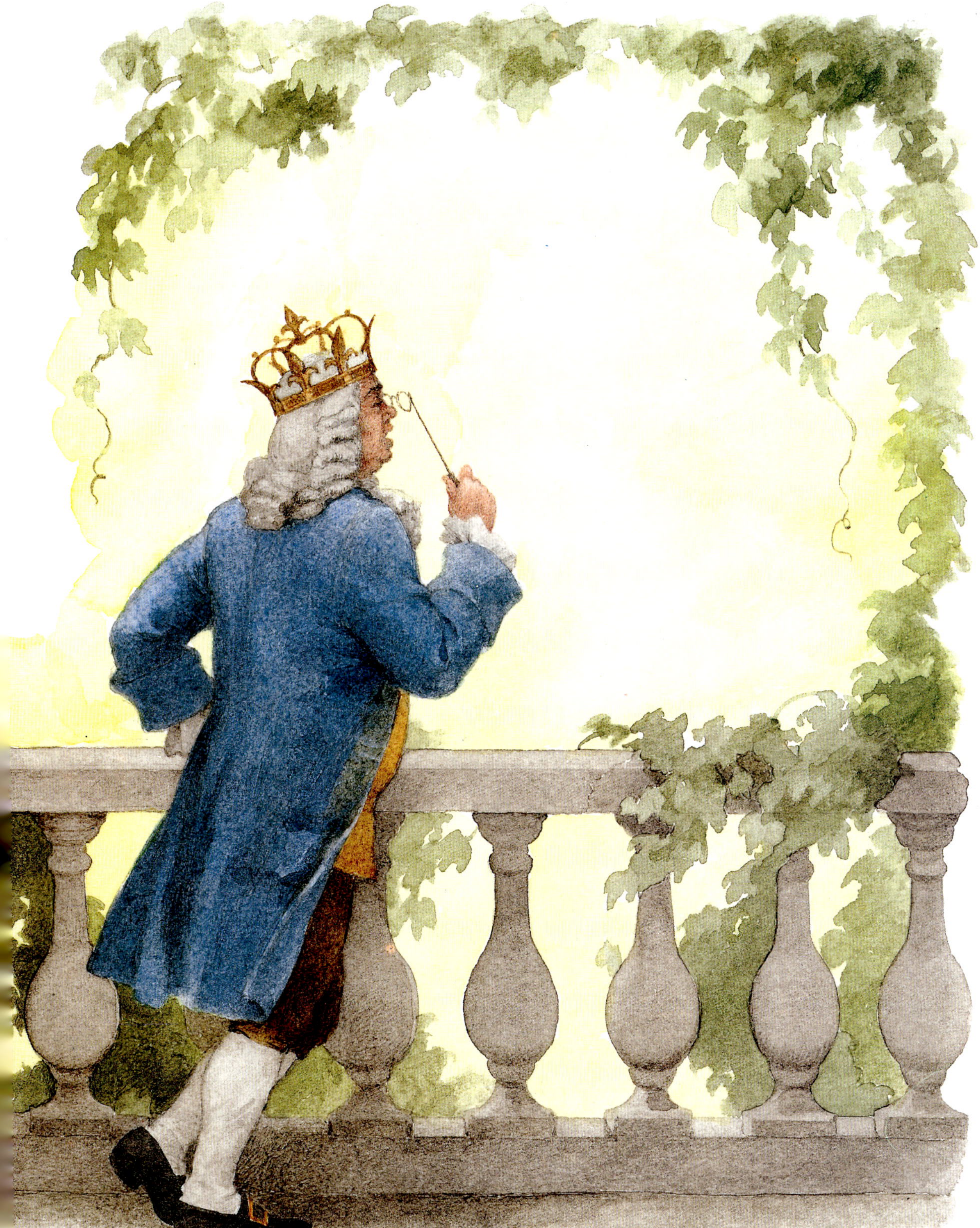

"Whatever's this?" he said, when he saw them kissing.

Then the emperor swiped them over the head with his slipper, just as the swineherd was having his eighty-sixth kiss.

"Get out!" cried the emperor, for he was wild. And both the swineherd and the princess were turned out of his kingdom. And so there she stood, crying, with the swineherd scolding her.

"Oh, how miserable I am!" said the princess. "If only I'd taken the handsome prince! Oh, I'm so unhappy!"

And, going behind a tree, the swineherd wiped the black and brown off his face, threw away his nasty clothes, and stepped forward in his prince's dress, looking so handsome that the princess curtsied when she saw him.

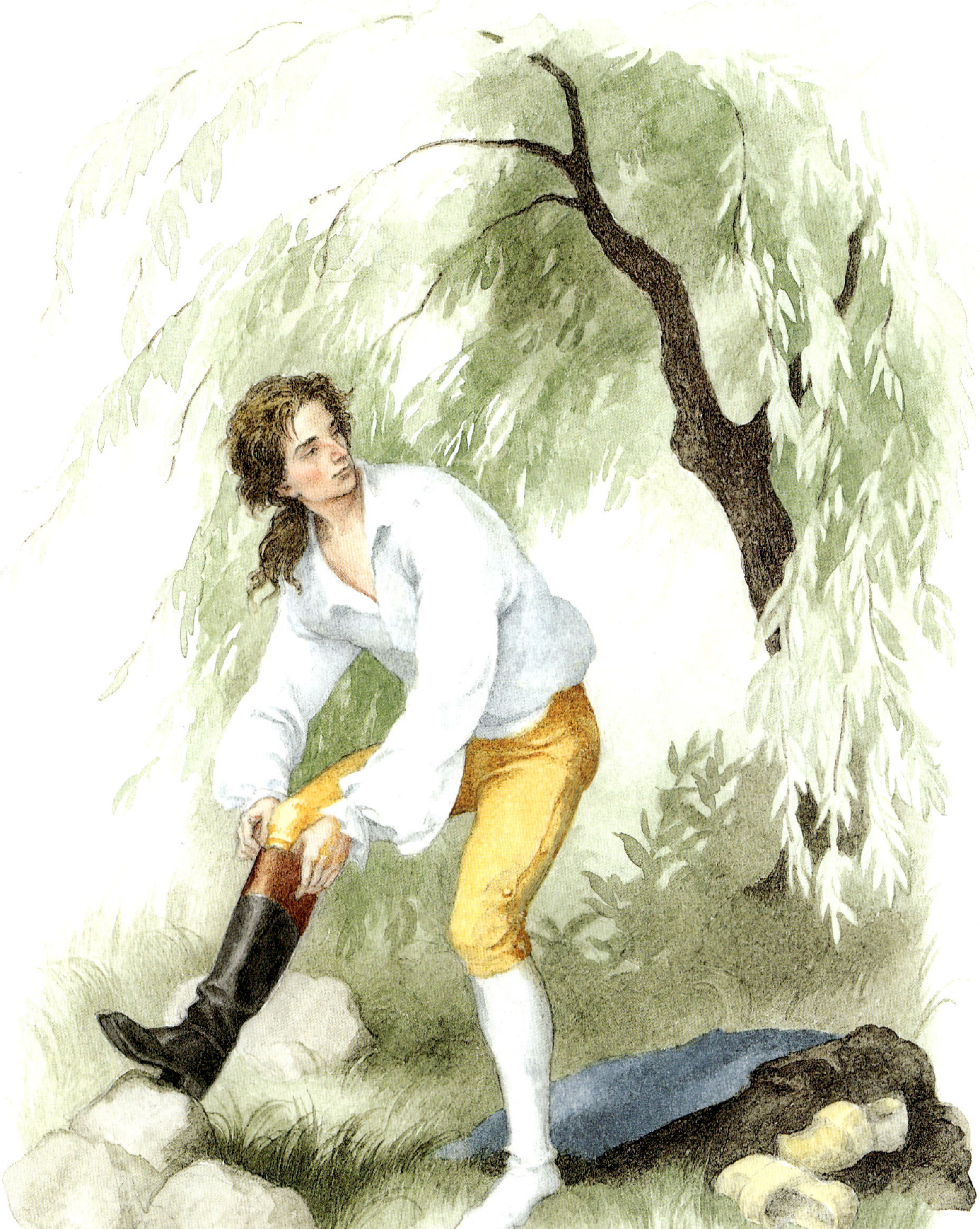

"I've learnt to despise you, my dear!" he said. "You wouldn't have an honest prince! The rose and the nightingale meant nothing to you! But the swineherd you could kiss for a musical-box! Now you can make the best of it!"

And going into his kingdom, he shut and bolted the door, leaving her standing outside to sing away to her heart's content:

"Ah, my darling Augustine,
Everything's lost, lost, lost!"

The Princess and the Pea

ONCE upon a time there was a prince who wanted to marry a princess; but she would have to be a real princess. He travelled all over the world to find one, but nowhere could he get what he wanted. There were princesses enough, but it was difficult to find out whether they were real ones. There was always something about them that was not as it should be. So he came home again and was sad, for he would have liked very much to have a real princess.

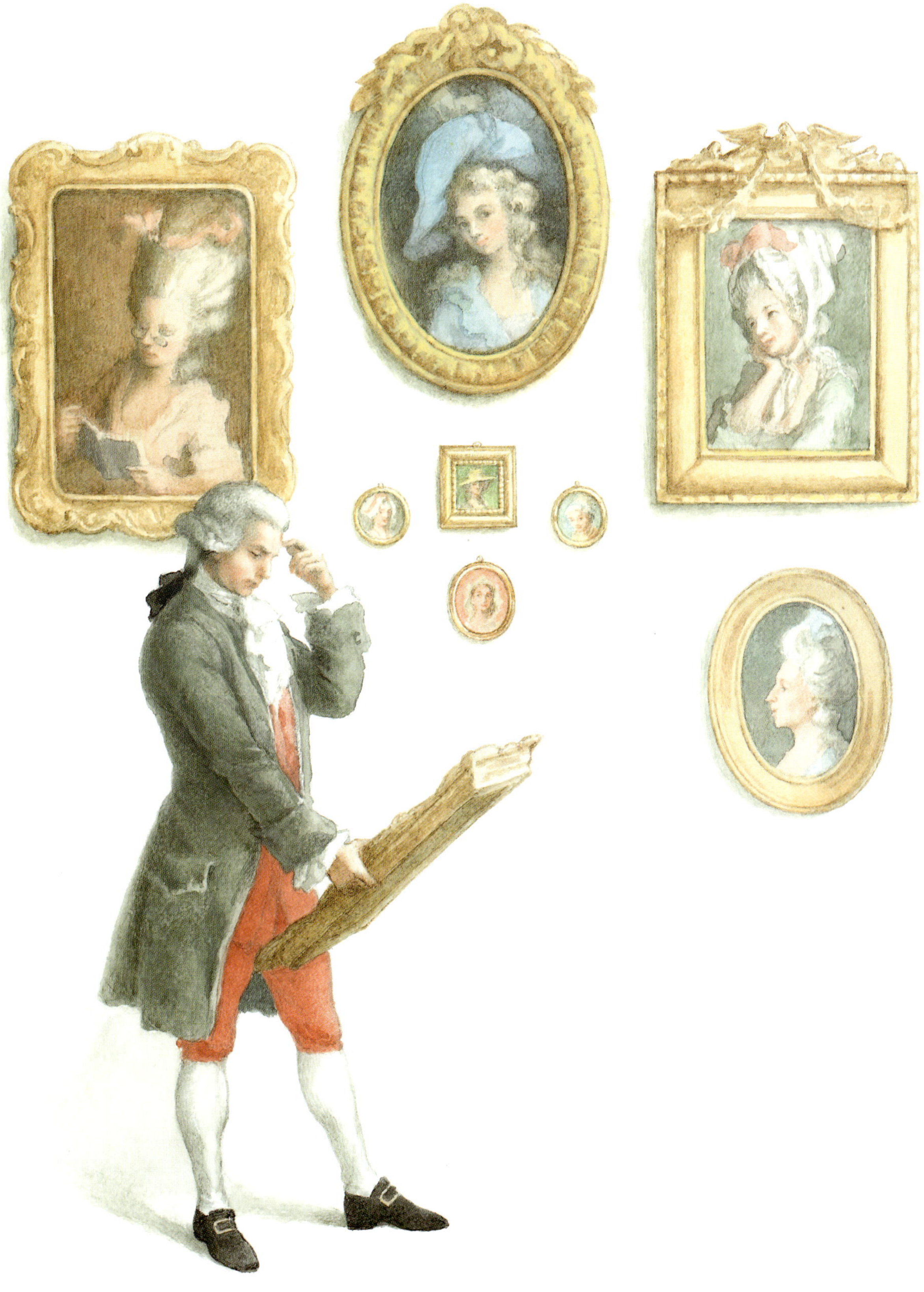

One evening a terrible storm came on; there was thunder and lightning, and the rain poured down in torrents. Suddenly a knocking was heard at the city gate, and the old king went to open it.

It was a princess standing out there in front of the gate. But, good gracious! what a sight the rain and the wind had made of her. The water ran down from her hair and clothes; it ran into the toes of her shoes and out again at the heels. Yet she said she was a real princess.

"Well, we'll soon find out about that," thought the old queen. But she said nothing, went into the bedroom, took all the bedding off the bedstead, and laid a pea on the bottom; then she took twenty mattresses and laid them on the pea, and then twenty eiderdowns on top of the mattresses.

On this the princess had to lie all night. In the morning she was asked how she had slept.

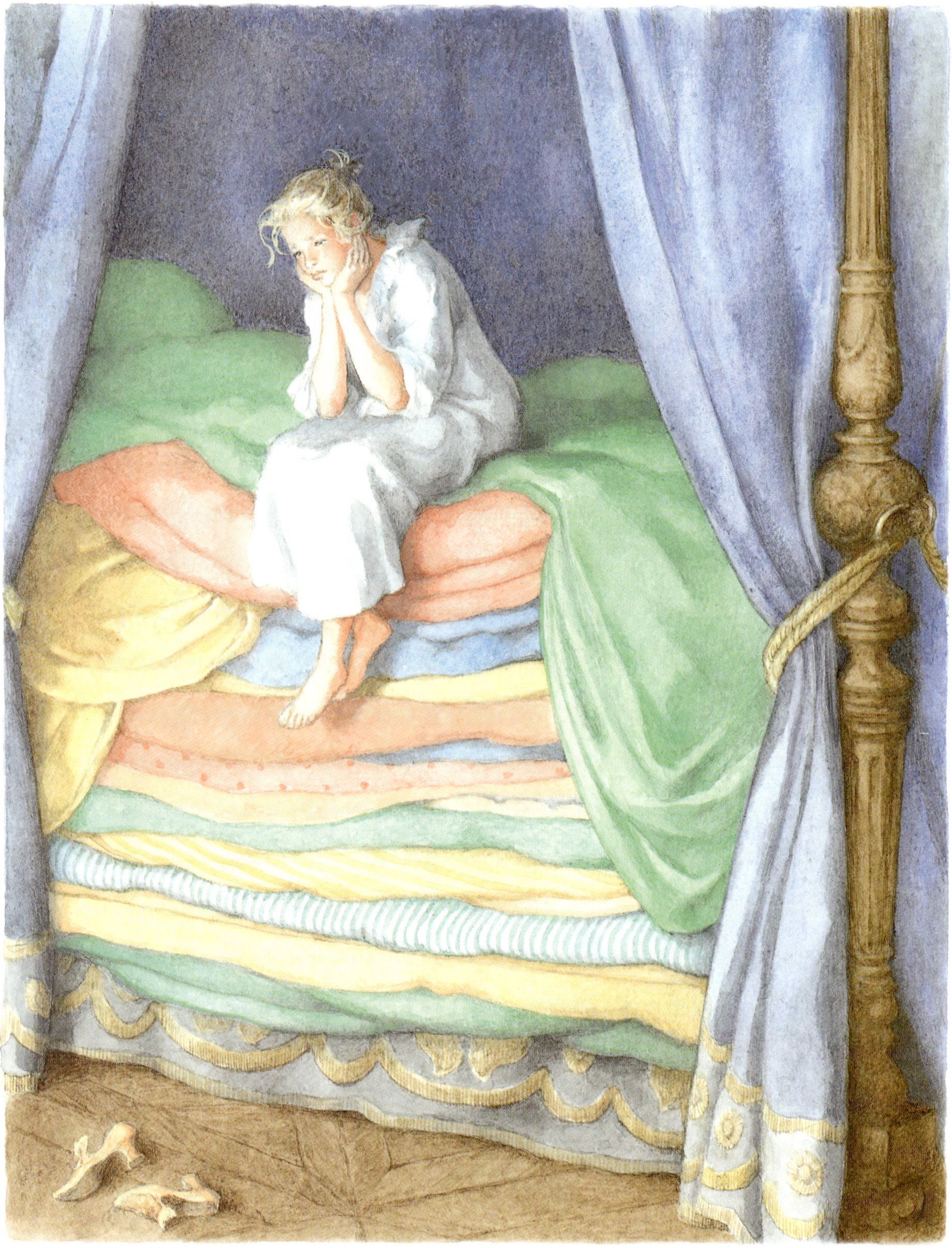

"Oh, very badly!" said she. "I hardly closed my eyes all night. Heaven only knows what was in the bed, but I was lying on something so hard that now I'm black and blue all over!"

Now they knew that she was a real princess because she had felt the pea right through the twenty mattresses and the twenty eiderdowns. Nobody but a real princess could be as sensitive as that.

So the prince took her for his wife, for now he knew that he had a real princess; and the pea was put in the museum, where it may still be seen, if no one has stolen it.

There, that is a true story.

The Snow Queen

A fairy tale in seven stories

First story:

The looking glass and the broken bits

THE story starts with a wicked imp, one of the wickedest of them all! One day he was in a very good humour. He had made a looking-glass with the magic power of making anything good and beautiful that looked into it shrink to nothing, while everything bad and ugly simply grew even worse. If they looked in it, even the nicest people became so nasty you wouldn't recognize them. This was great fun, thought the wicked imp.

All the other imps said that for the first time, you could see what human beings really looked like. They ran about all over the world with the looking-glass, doing mischief everywhere.

Then the imps thought they would fly up to Heaven and make fun of the angels. But the higher they flew with the looking-glass, the harder it was for them to hold on to it. As they flew higher and higher, all at once the looking-glass shot out of their hands and crashed to earth, where it broke into billions of pieces of glass.

Now this caused even more mischief than before; for many of the bits were smaller than a grain of sand, and these all went flying round the world. As each tiny splinter had the same power as the whole looking-glass, if it got into someone's eyes, it would stick there and make them have an eye only for what was bad. And if anyone got a little bit in their hearts, that was really dreadful, for then their hearts became like a lump of ice. Larger pieces of glass were used to make spectacles which made everything go wrong when people put them on. The wicked imp laughed till his sides split. Meanwhile millions of little bits went on floating in the air. Now listen to what happened to one of them.

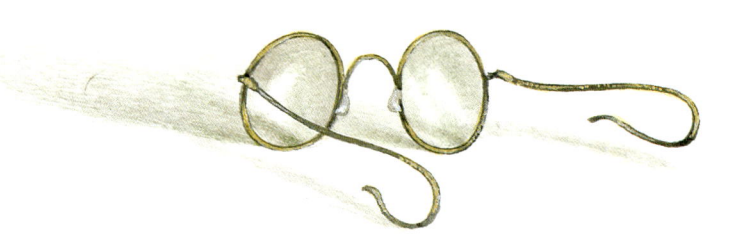

Second Story: A little boy and a little girl

In the middle of the city, there lived two poor children who loved each other like brother and sister. He was called Kay and she was called Gerda. They lived in next-door houses with their rooms under the eaves. A little window opened out from each gable. You only had to step across in order to get from one window to the other.

Here where the parents had a little roof garden with rose-bushes, the children would sit together on summer days, reading or playing happily. In winter, they played indoors. The attic windows would often be quite frozen; then they would warm pennies by the stove and, pressing them on the glass, make little peepholes to look out at the falling snow.

"That's the swarming of the white bees," said Granny.

"Have they a queen bee as well?" asked Kay.

"Why, yes!" said Granny. "She flies with the swarm! On winter nights she peeps in at the windows, and then they freeze up all strangely, just like flowers."

"Yes, we've seen it!" cried the two children.

"Can the Snow Queen come inside?" asked the little girl.

"Just let her come," said the boy, "and I'll put her on the hot stove and make her melt." But Granny smoothed his hair and told them other stories.

One winter's evening, Kay climbed up to the window and peeped out. Snow was falling and a large snowflake came to rest on the edge of the roof. The snowflake grew and grew until Kay saw it was a woman, dressed in the finest gauze, made up of millions of starry flakes. She herself was so pretty and delicate, yet was made of glittering ice. Her eyes gazed like bright stars, never still or resting. She nodded to him and waved her hand. At that, Kay was frightened and jumped down.

A few days later, Kay and Gerda were looking at a picture-book when — just as the clock in the church tower struck five — Kay said: "Oh, something pricked me! And now I've got something in my eye!"

Gerda put her arms round him and looked closely while he blinked; but no, there was nothing to be seen.

"I think it's gone!" Kay said. But it hadn't. It was a tiny splinter of glass from the wicked imp's looking-glass. Poor Kay had a bit right in his heart; soon it would be like a lump of ice.

"Why are you crying?" he asked impatiently. "It makes you look ugly! There's nothing wrong with me!"

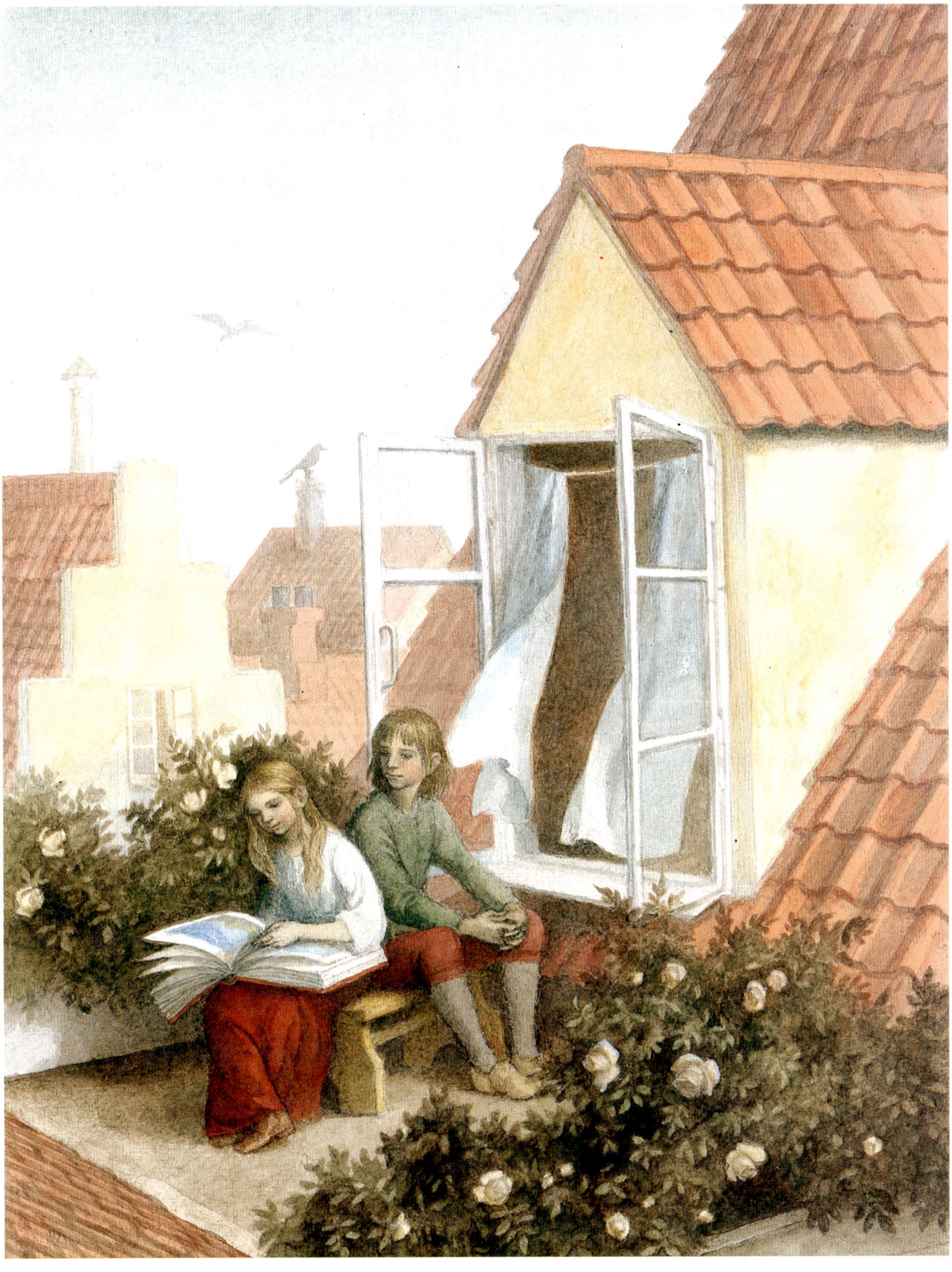

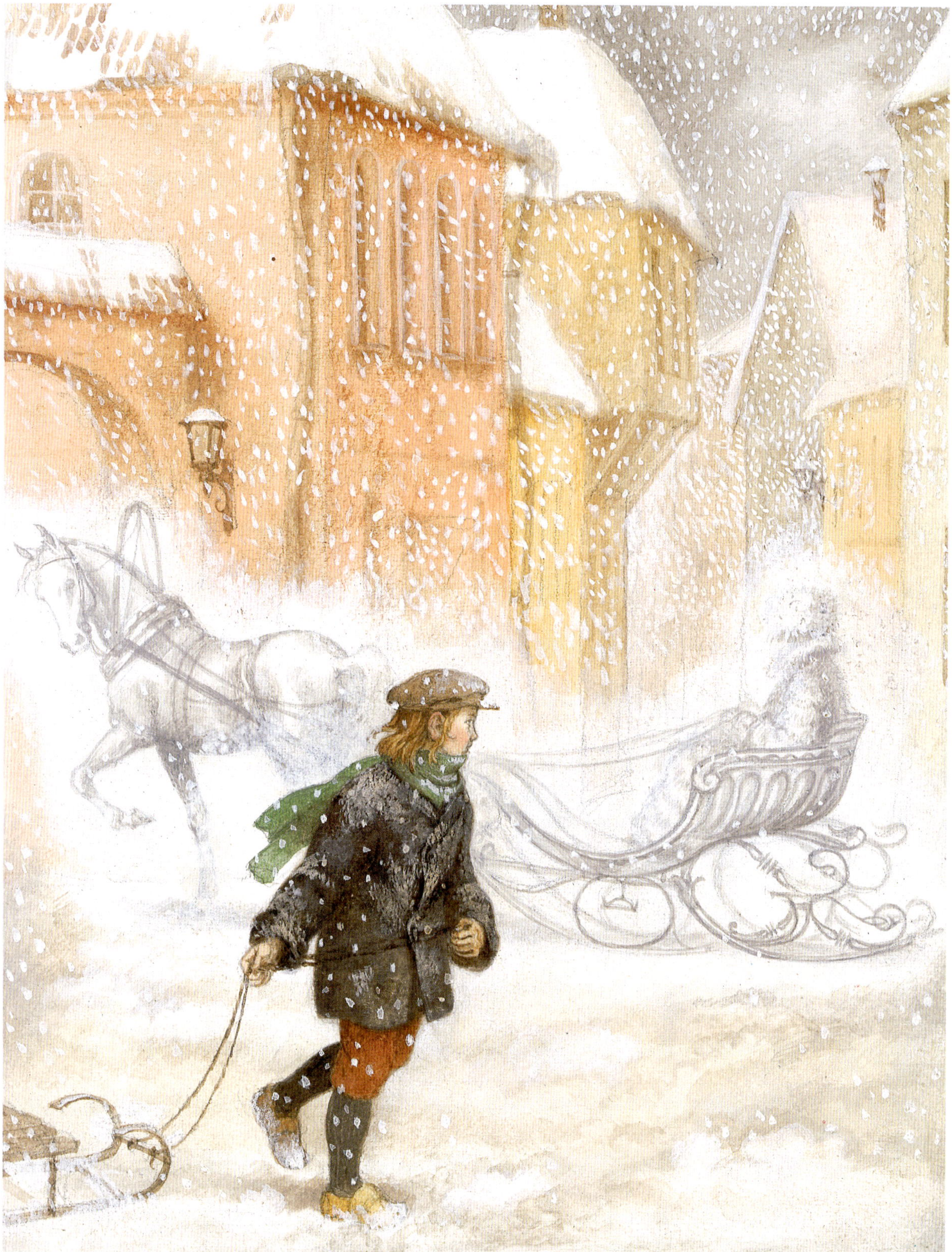

When Gerda showed him the book again, Kay said it was babyish. He seemed so different, Gerda hardly knew him.

The next day, Kay appeared carrying his sledge. He shouted to Gerda: "I'm allowed to go and sledge on the square with the other boys!" And with that he was off.

The boys were all playing on the square when along came a big white sleigh. The person driving it was wrapped in a white fur cloak and cap. As the sleigh drove slowly round, Kay tied his sledge to the back for fun — like the older boys did — and was pulled along. Faster and faster it went, the driver turning round and giving Kay a nod as if they knew each other. They drove out through the city gates. And then the snow began falling so fast that Kay couldn't see in front of him as they tore along. He tried to loose the rope from the sleigh, but it was of no use; his sledge was tied fast and travelling like the wind. He shouted; but the sleigh only went racing on.

Then all at once the sleigh stopped, and the driver got up. It was a lady, tall, straight and all gleaming white. It was the Snow Queen.

"Why, you're cold!" she said. "Come, wrap yourself in my bearskin cloak!"

She sat him beside her in the big white sleigh, and put her cloak round him; it felt like sinking in a snowdrift.

"Do you still feel cold?" she asked, kissing him on the forehead. Her kiss was colder than ice and went straight to his heart, which was already half ice. The Snow Queen kissed Kay once more, and by this time he had forgotten little Gerda and everyone at home.

They flew over woods and lakes, over seas and lands. The cold wind whistled and the snow glittered; up above the moon shone clear and Kay watched it all the long winter's night. During the day he slept at the Snow Queen's feet.

Third Story: The woman who worked magic

Spring came round at last, bringing warmer sunshine.

"Kay's dead and gone!" said little Gerda to the swallows.

"We don't think so!" they all said.

"I'm going to put on my new red shoes," she said. "And then I'll go and ask the river!" Early next morning, she put on her red shoes and went through the city gate and down to the river.

"Have you taken my playmate, Kay?" she asked. "I'll give you my new shoes if you'll return him to me!"

The waves seemed to nod so strangely to her that she took her shoes and threw them into the river, but they floated straight back. She thought she hadn't thrown the shoes far enough and so, climbing to the end of a boat which lay there, she threw the shoes out again. The boat wasn't tied up, and it started to float away from the bank.

Although Gerda was quite frightened, she thought to herself: "Perhaps the river will take me to Kay!" And cheered by this she stood up and gazed at the beautiful green banks. In time she came by a curious little thatched house with two wooden soldiers outside.

Gerda called out and an old, old woman came from the house, leaning on a crooked stick.

"You poor child!" said the old woman. "However did you come to be drifting away into the wide, wide world?" And hooking her crooked stick on to the boat, she pulled it ashore and lifted Gerda out. And Gerda was glad to be on dry land, though a bit afraid of the strange old woman.

Then Gerda told her story, and asked the old woman if she had seen little Kay, and the woman said no, but he was sure to come; meanwhile, she should cheer up and must taste her cherries, and enjoy her lovely flower-garden. And while Gerda was eating her cherries, the old woman combed her hair with a golden comb till it curled and shone.

"How I've longed for a little girl like you!" said the old woman. "Now just you see how well we two are going to get on!" And as her hair was combed, Gerda forgot all about Kay; for the old woman could work magic, though she wasn't a wicked witch. She simply wished to keep little Gerda with her.

Time passed, and soon Gerda was allowed into the garden to enjoy the flowers in the warm sunshine. The most beautiful of all was a rose-bush. One day Gerda sat by it and, thinking of the lovely roses at home in the roof garden, she remembered Kay.

"Oh, I must find Kay!" cried Gerda. "Do you think he's dead and gone?" she asked the roses.

"He isn't dead!" they said. "We were in the ground all winter. That's where the dead are, but Kay wasn't there!"

Gerda ran to the garden gate and shook the rusty latch till it came loose and the gate sprang open. And then Gerda ran in her bare feet into the wide world. At last she couldn't run any longer and sat down on a big stone.

"Why, it's autumn already! Oh, dear, how I've wasted my time!" said Gerda. "Now I daren't rest!" And she got up to go.

Fourth Story: The prince and princess

Gerda travelled on for what seemed a very long time. One day as she rested, a big crow hopped in front of her. It wagged its head, and said: "Caw! Caw!" Gerda told the crow her story and asked if it had seen Kay.

The crow said thoughtfully: "Perhaps I have. It may be Kay! But I rather think he's forgotten you now for the princess!"

"Does he live with a princess?" asked Gerda.

"Why, yes!" said the crow. "In this kingdom lives a princess who's very clever. She was sitting on the throne last week when she thought: 'Why shouldn't I get married?'

"She told her ladies in waiting, and they were all delighted. They declared that any handsome young man was free to come and talk to the princess, and the one who talked best would be her husband. Well," said the crow, "people flocked to the palace."

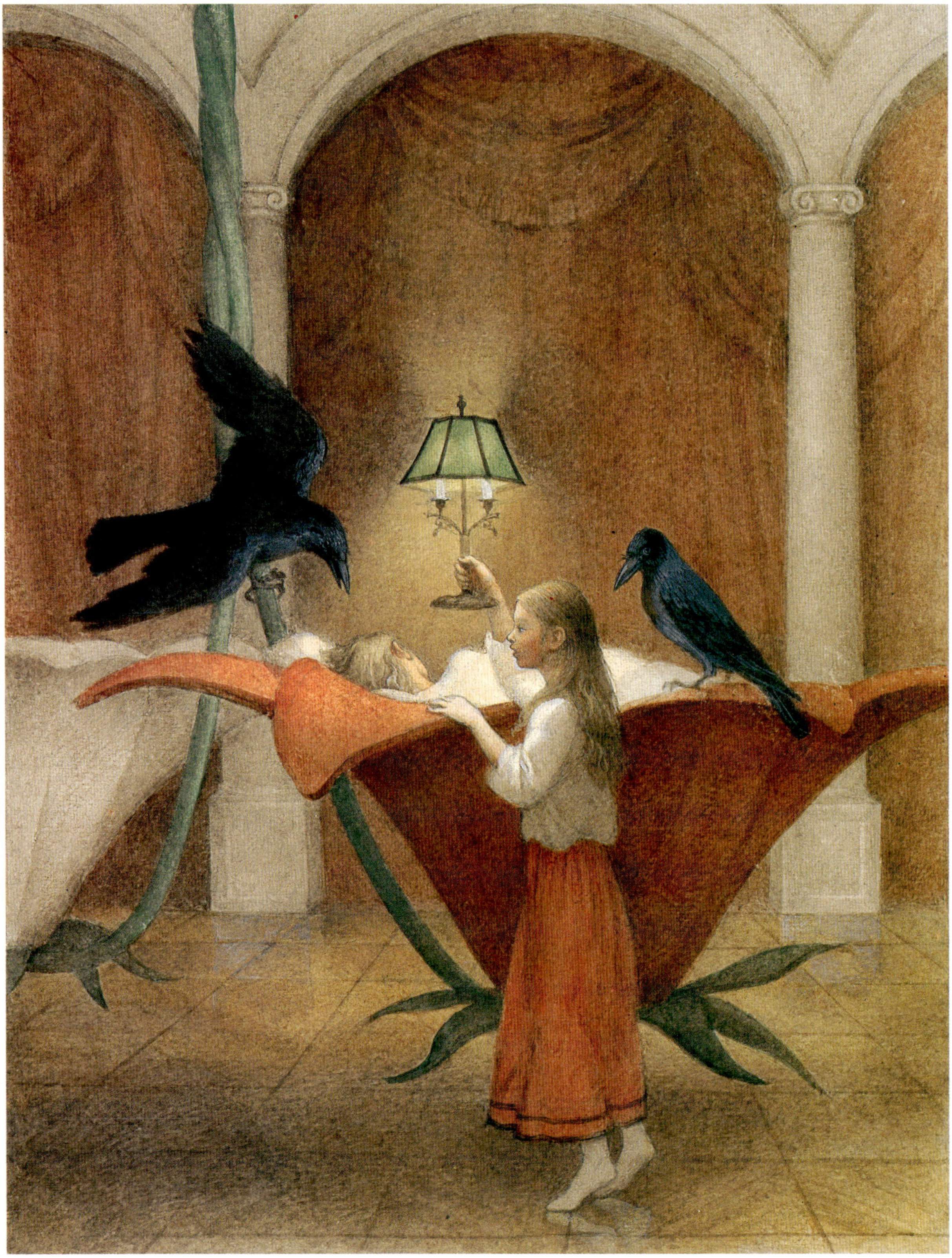

"But Kay?" asked Gerda. "Was he among them?"

"Hold on! I'm coming to that! Yesterday a little fellow came marching up. His eyes shone like yours and he had lovely long hair, but poor clothes."

"That was Kay!" cried Gerda, delighted. "And he won the princess?"

"She thought he talked the best," said the crow.

"Why, of course it was Kay," said Gerda. "He is so clever. Oh, please will you take me to the palace?"

"A child with bare feet will never be admitted," said the crow. "But don't despair. My sweetheart knows a secret way in. Wait here," said the crow, and flew off.

At nightfall, the crow returned with his sweetheart. They went into the palace garden, and the crows took Gerda to a little back door and up the stairs. At last they were in a bedchamber, where there were two beds shaped like lilies. One of them was white, and here lay the princess. In the other there lay a young man. Yes, it was Kay! She called his name and held up a lamp. He woke, turned, and — it wasn't Kay. The prince only resembled Kay, being young and handsome.

Waking in her white bed, the princess asked what was the matter. And little Gerda wept and told her story and what the crows had done for her.

"You poor thing," they said. And the prince got up and let Gerda sleep in his bed, she looked so very weary.

The next day she was dressed all in silk and velvet, with warm boots and a muff. A coach of pure gold stood at the door, full of sugar biscuits, fruit and ginger-nuts. The prince and the princess helped her into the carriage and wished her good luck.

"Goodbye!, Goodbye!" they cried, and the crows flew up into a tree, and flapped their black wings as long as the coach was in sight.

Fifth Story: The little robber girl

They drove through the dark forest, where the golden coach shone like fire and caught the robbers' eyes.

"Gold! Gold!" they cried; rushing forward, they seized the horses, killed the coachman and then pulled little Gerda out of the coach.

"She's plump, she's been fattened on nuts!" said an old robber woman, drawing out her sharp knife. Then suddenly she cried out for she had been bitten by her own daughter, who was as wild and mischievous as anything.

"She'll play with me," cried the little robber girl. "I want to go in the coach with her." And she got her own way, she was so spoilt and self-willed.

She and Gerda got in and away they drove. The little robber girl was the same age as Gerda but stronger and dark-skinned. With her arm round Gerda, she said: "I suppose you're a princess."

"No," said Gerda, and she told her all her adventures.

The robber girl looked at her and said: "They shan't kill you; I'll see that I do it myself." And drying Gerda's eyes, she put her hands into the warm muff.

The coach soon arrived at the robbers' castle. In the big hall, soup was simmering over a large fire, and meat was turning on spits.

"You shall sleep here with me and all my pets!" said the robber girl. They ate and drank, and then went into a corner, where there were blankets and straw. Up above there were nearly a hundred pigeons sleeping.

"They're all mine," said the robber girl. "And this is my old Baa-baa!" She tugged the horn of a reindeer, which was tied up. "Every night I tickle his neck with my knife; that frightens him!"

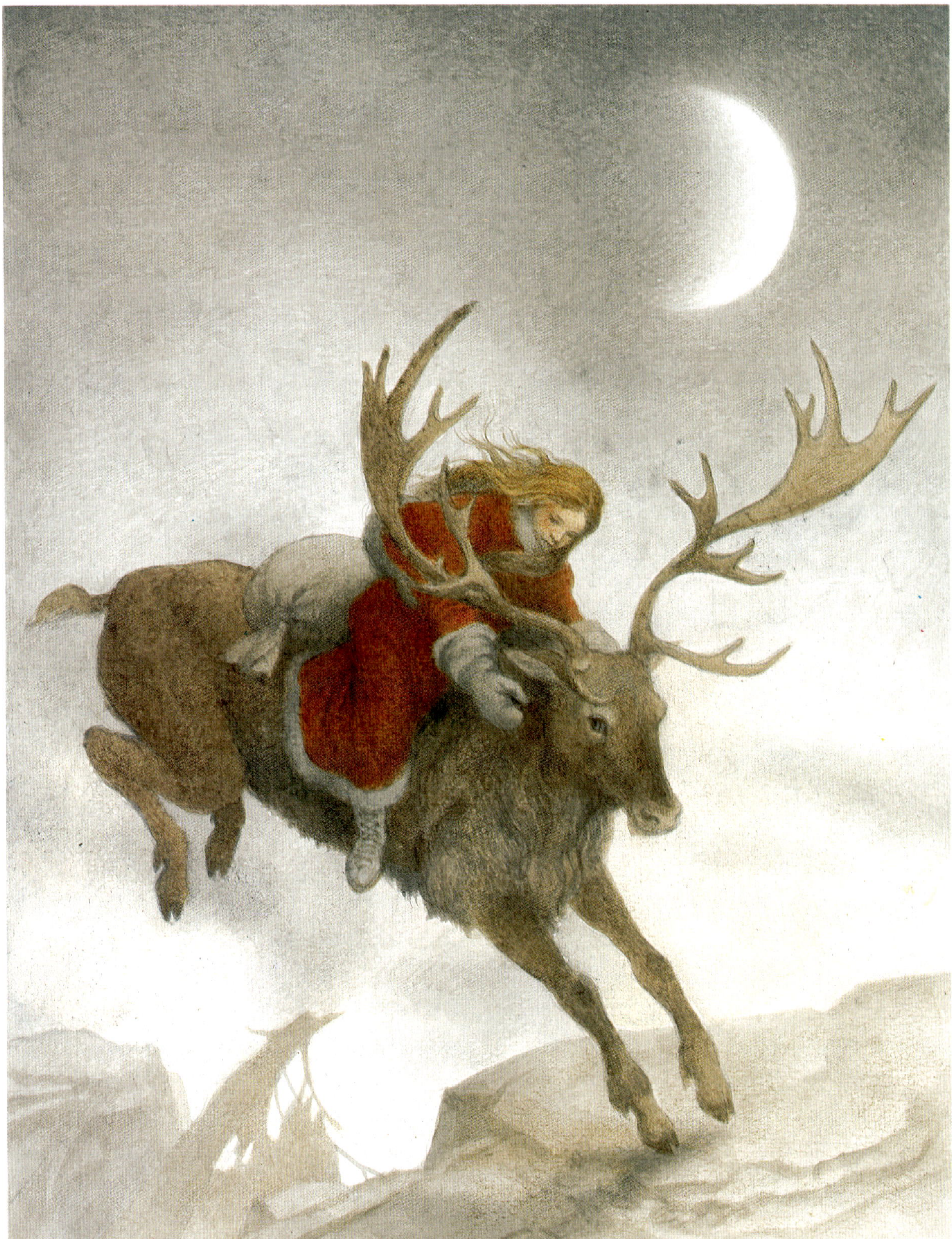

And she ran her knife over the reindeer's neck. The poor creature backed in fear, but the girl only laughed.

"Now," said the robber girl, "tell me again about Kay."

So Gerda told her again while two wood pigeons in a cage went on cooing above. Then the robber girl put her arms round Gerda and fell fast asleep. But Gerda couldn't sleep a wink, not knowing if she would live or die.

All at once the wood-pigeons called: "Coo! Coo! We've seen little Kay. He was in the Snow Queen's carriage."

"What's that?" cried Gerda. "Where did they go?"

"They went towards Lapland, where there's always snow."

"Oh, Kay, Kay!" sighed Gerda, as she lay sleepless.

In the morning Gerda told the robber girl what the wood-pigeons had said, and she looked very serious, but then asked the reindeer: "Do you know where Lapland is?"

"I was born there," said the animal, its eyes sparkling.

The robber girl said: "I love tickling you with my knife. But I'll let you go, so you can take this little girl to the Snow Queen's palace."

The reindeer leapt for joy. The robber girl lifted Gerda up, tied her fast and even gave her a little cushion.

"Take my mother's big mittens," she said, "for it will be cold. Hands in!"

Stretching out her hands in the big mittens to the robber girl, Gerda said good-bye, and the reindeer flew off through the forest and over swamps and plains for all it was worth. And soon they were in Lapland.

Sixth Story: The Lapp woman and the Finn woman

They came to a stop at a wretched little house where there was nobody but an old Lapp woman frying fish at an oil-lamp. The reindeer told her Gerda's whole story as Gerda was too cold to speak.

"Oh, you poor things!" said the Lapp woman. "You've got hundreds of miles to go yet, right into Finnmark. I'll write a note on a piece of dried cod for you to take to the Finn woman. She'll tell you more than I can!"

And so when Gerda had eaten and warmed up, the Lapp woman wrote a few words on a piece of dried cod, tied Gerda on to the reindeer again, and off it sprang. The loveliest blue Northern Lights burnt all night long. And so they came to Finnmark, where they knocked at the Finn woman's chimney, for she didn't have a door.

Inside it was so hot that the Finn woman herself wore few clothes. She was a little woman, and rather grubby. She took off Gerda's mittens and boots, read the message on the dried cod three times and put the fish in the cooking-pot. Then she drew the reindeer aside and whispered:

"Little Kay is with the Snow Queen sure enough, and there he is perfectly content. But that's because he's got a splinter of glass in his heart and another in his eye. They'll have to come out, or he'll never be human again and the Snow Queen will have him in her power."

"Can't you give Gerda something, so that she'll have power, too."

"I can't give her any greater power than she already has! Don't you see how well she has got on in the world, in her bare feet? It's in her heart! She's

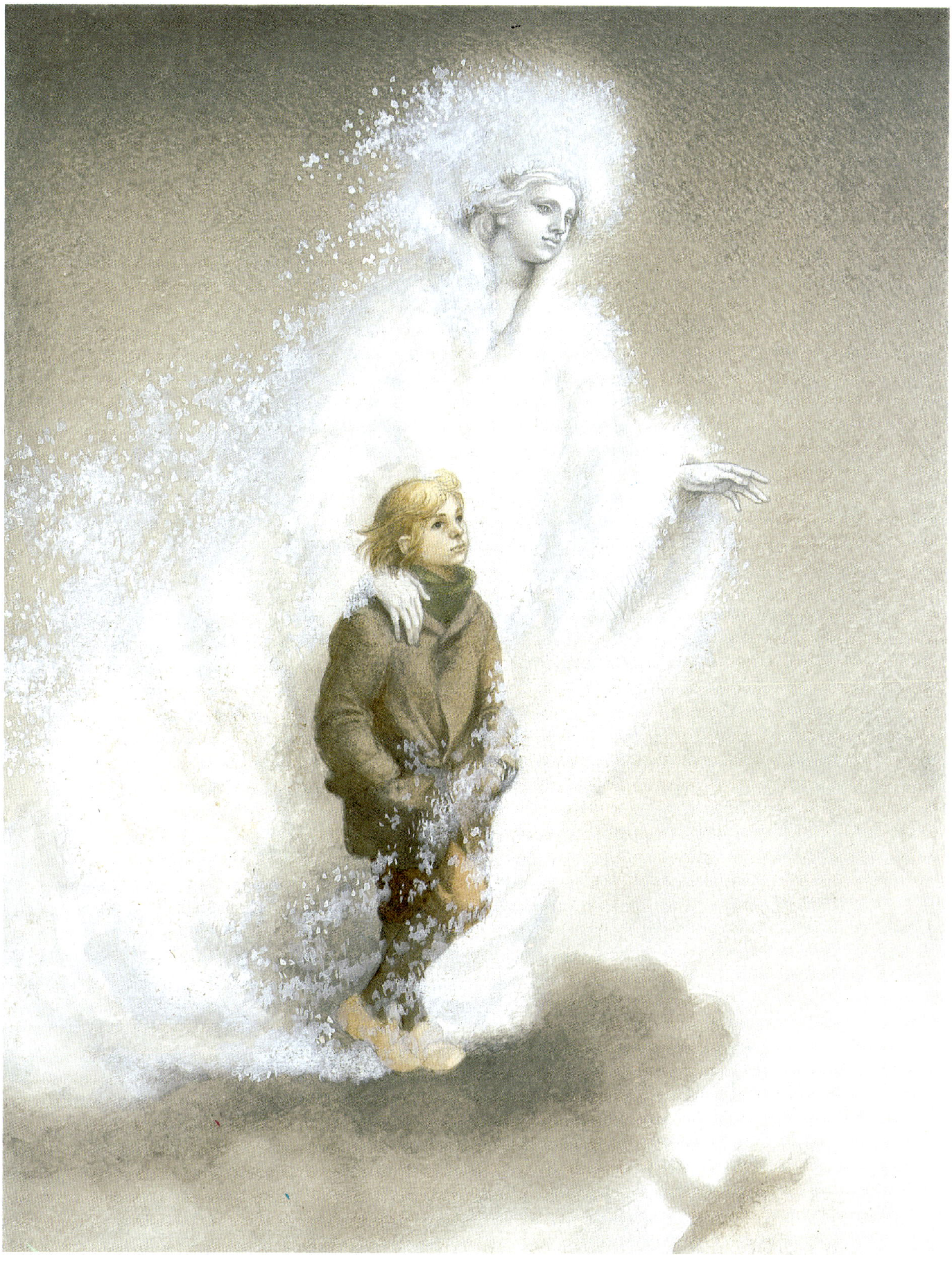

a sweet and innocent child. If she can't find her way to the Snow Queen and get the glass out of little Kay, then we can't help her! Ten miles from here is the edge of the Snow Queen's garden; leave the little girl by the berry bush there." So saying the Finn woman lifted Gerda on to the reindeer, which ran off as fast as its legs would carry it.

"Oh, I didn't get my boots! I didn't get my mittens!" cried Gerda. She could feel the biting cold. But the reindeer ran on till it came to the Snow Queen's garden. There it kissed Gerda while tears rolled down the creature's cheeks. Then it left poor Gerda there, without shoes, without gloves, in the middle of dreadful, icy-cold Finnmark.

She ran on, and soon met a whole regiment of snowflakes; but they didn't fall from the sky. They were running, and the nearer they came the bigger they grew: they were the Snow Queen's sentries!

Now Gerda said her prayers. The cold was so fierce that she could see her own breath like a cloud of smoke; denser and denser it grew, until it took the form of bright little angels that went on growing. Every one wore a helmet and carried a sword and a shield. More and more came, until there was a whole army. And they set about the snowflakes and broke them into a hundred pieces, allowing Gerda to walk safely on. And the angels stroked her feet and hands, so that she didn't feel the cold as she walked on to the Snow Queen's palace.

Seventh Story: What happened in the Snow Queen's palace

The palace walls were of drifting snow, the windows and doors of cutting winds. There were over a hundred halls; the biggest stretched for many miles. All were lit up by the fierce Northern Lights, and were so large, so empty, so icy-cold. Here, Kay was quite blue with cold; though he never felt it. His heart was as a lump of ice. The Snow Queen had flown off to touch the mountains up with white, and Kay sat all by himself in the bare hall, stiff and silent.

Then Gerda entered the palace, through the big gates of biting winds. There she saw Kay. She knew him at once and flung her arms round his neck, holding him tight and crying: "Kay! Dear Kay!"

But he sat perfectly still and stiff and cold. Seeing this, Gerda shed hot tears and they fell on his breast and went through to his heart, where they melted the lump of ice and swallowed up the glass splinter. Then Kay burst into tears;

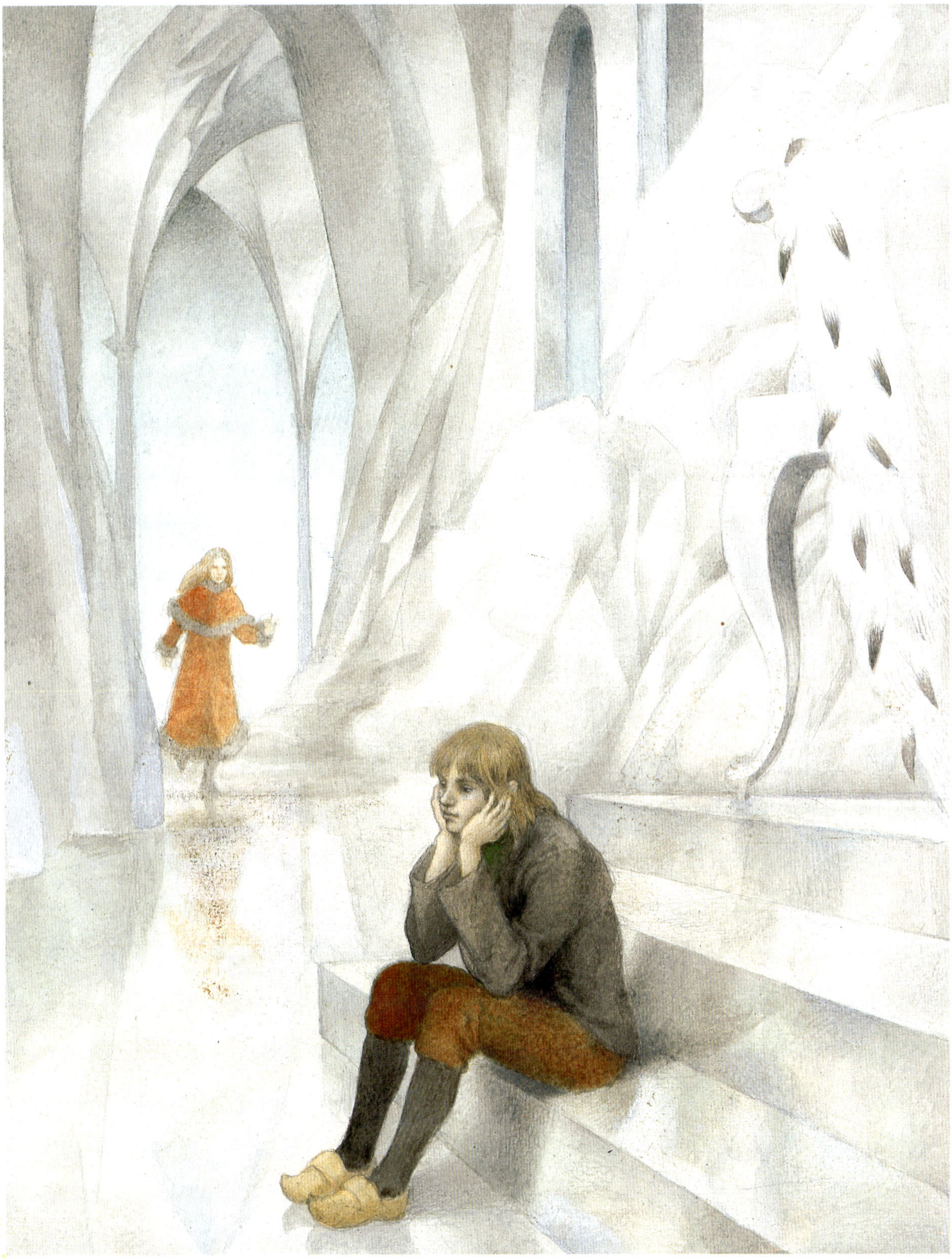

and wept till the bit of glass fell out of his eye, when he knew her again and cried for joy:

"Gerda! Dear Gerda! Where have you been all this long time? And where have I been?"

Then, looking round him, he said: "How cold and bare it is!" And he held Gerda tight while she cried and laughed for joy. Then Gerda kissed his cheeks and they became rosy. She kissed his eyes and they shone like hers; she kissed his hands and feet and he was well and strong.

And taking each other by the hand, they walked out of the big hall. They talked of home, of Granny and the roses in the roof garden, and wherever they went, the winds dropped and the sun broke through. And when they got to the berry bush, there waiting for them was the reindeer which carried Kay and Gerda first to the Finn woman's where they warmed themselves, and then to the Lapp woman who had got ready her sledge.

The reindeer ran alongside as far as the country's border; there, where the first green things peeped up from the ground, they said goodbye. And the birds began to sing, the wood was in bud and there on a splendid horse came a young girl with a red cap on her head and pistols in front. It was the little robber girl who was tired of staying at home. She knew Gerda at once and Gerda knew her. They were delighted. And taking them both by the hands, she promised that if ever she visited their town she would call and see them. And with that she rode off into the wide world.

Kay and Gerda went on hand in hand and everywhere were flowers and everything green. The church bells were ringing as they came to their own town. And they walked into the house where everything stood where it had stood before, Granny sat reading from the Bible and the clock still said "Tick! Tick!" But as they walked in at the door they felt that they had become grown-up people. Now Kay and Gerda had forgotten, like a bad dream, the cold empty splendour at the Snow Queen's palace. The roses were blooming by the open windows, and it was summer, warm and blessed summer.

The Emperor's New Suit

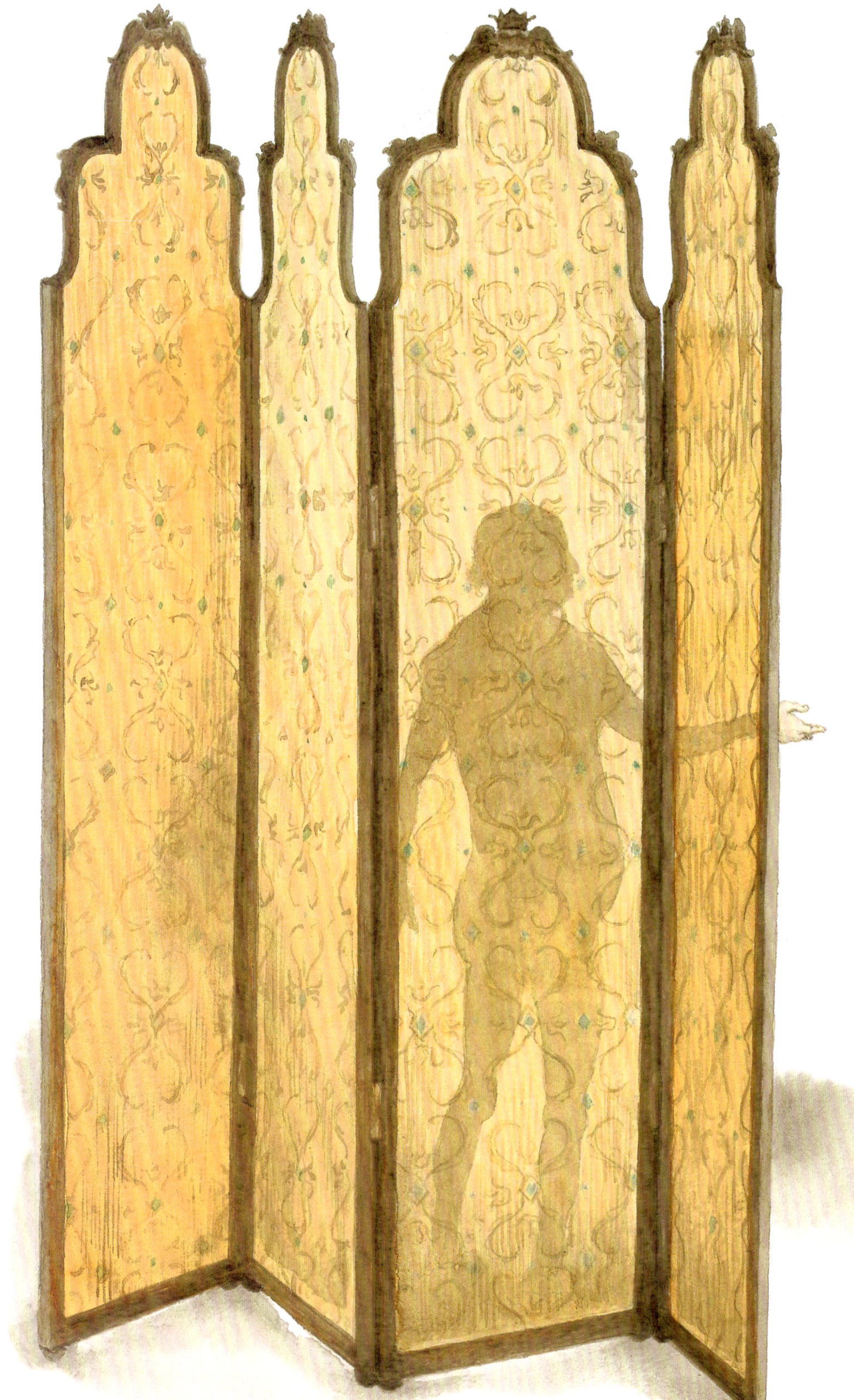

Many, many years ago lived an emperor, who thought so much of new clothes that he spent all his money in order to be always well dressed. He did not care for his soldiers, and the theatre did not amuse him; the only thing he thought anything of was to drive out and show off a new suit of clothes. He had a coat for every hour of the day; and just as one might say of a king "He is in his council chamber," so one said of the emperor, "He is in his dressing-room."

The great city where he resided was very merry. Every day visitors arrived from all parts, and among them, one day two swindlers arrived. They made people believe that they were weavers, and declared they could work the finest cloth to be imagined. Their colours and patterns, they said, were not only beautiful, but the clothes made of it possessed the wonderful quality of being invisible to any man who was stupid or unfit for his office.

"That must be wonderful cloth," thought the emperor. "If I were to be dressed in a suit made of this cloth I should be able to find out which men in my empire were unfit for their places, and I could distinguish the clever from the stupid. I must have this cloth woven for me without delay." And he gave a large sum of money to the swindlers, in advance, that they should set to work without any loss of time.

So they set up two looms, and pretended to be very hard at work, but they did nothing whatever on the looms. They asked for the finest silk and the most precious gold-cloth; all they got they did away with, and worked at the empty looms till late at night.

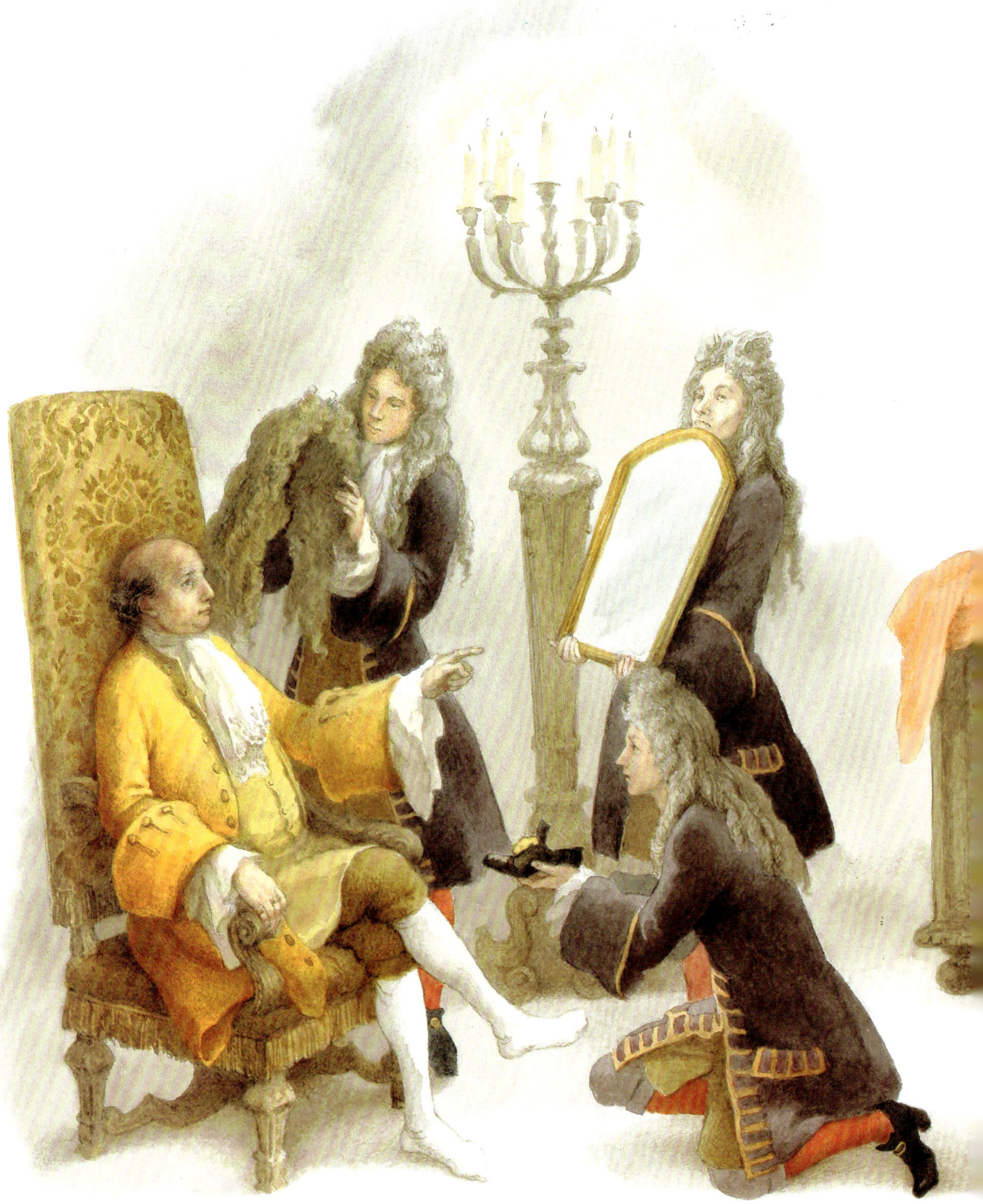

"I should very much like to know how they are getting on with the cloth," thought the emperor. But he felt rather uneasy when he remembered that anyone who wasn't fit for his office couldn't see it. He thought it advisable to send somebody else first to see how matters stood. Everybody in the town knew what a remarkable quality the cloth possessed, and all were anxious to see how bad or stupid their neighbours were.

"I shall send my honest old minister to the weavers," thought the emperor. "He can judge best how the cloth looks, for he is intelligent, and nobody understands his office better than he."

The good old minister went into the room where the swindlers sat before the empty looms. "Heaven preserve us!" he thought, and opened his eyes wide, "I cannot see anything at all," but he did not say so. Both swindlers requested him to come near, and asked him if he did not admire the exquisite pattern and the beautiful colours, pointing to the empty looms. The poor old minister tried his very best, but he could see nothing. "Oh dear," he thought, "can I be so stupid? Is it possible that I am not fit for my office? No, no, I cannot say that I was unable to see the cloth."

"Now, have you got nothing to say?" said one of the swindlers, while he pretended to be busily weaving.

"Oh, it is very pretty, exceedingly beautiful," replied the old minister looking through his glasses. "What a beautiful pattern, what brilliant colours! I shall tell the emperor that I like the cloth very much."

"We are pleased to hear that," said the two weavers, and described to him the colours and explained the curious pattern. The old minister listened attentively, that he might relate to the emperor what they said; and so he did.

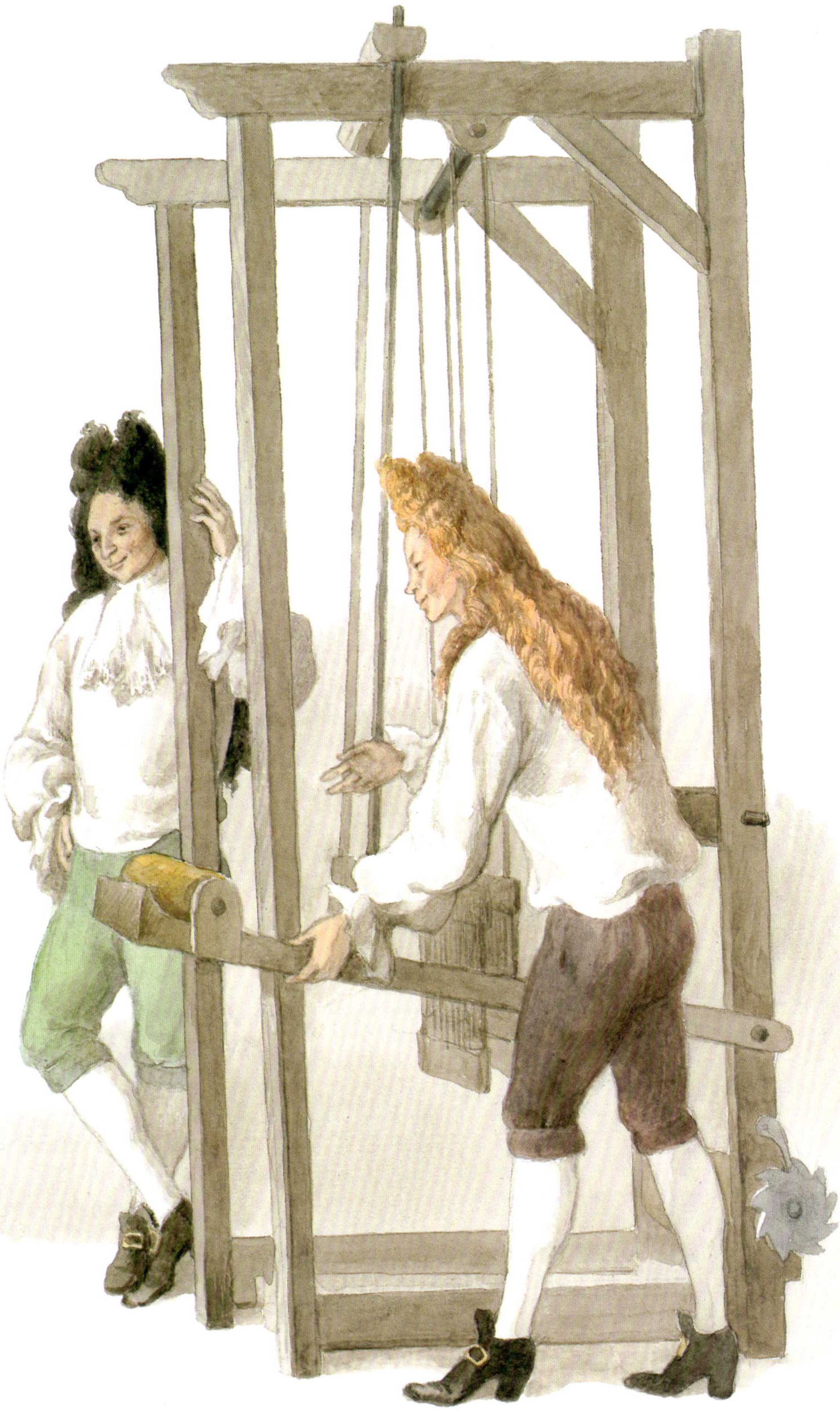

Now the swindlers asked for more money, silk and gold-cloth, which they required for weaving. They kept everything for themselves, and not a thread came near the loom, but they continued as before to work at the empty looms.

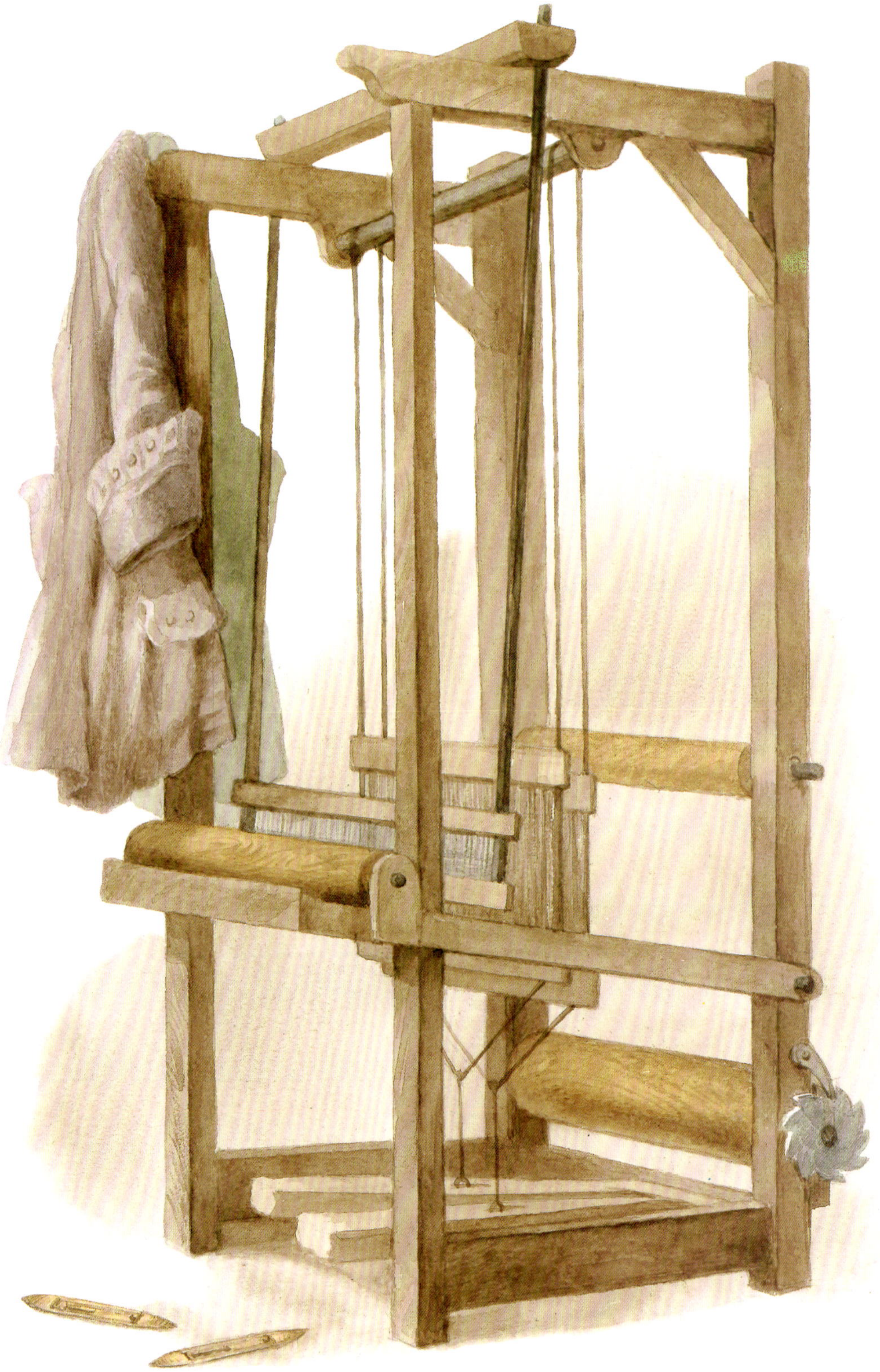

Soon afterwards the emperor sent another honest courtier to the weavers to see how they were getting on, and if the cloth was nearly finished. Like the old minister, he looked and looked but could see nothing, as there was nothing to be seen.

"Is it not a beautiful piece of cloth?" asked the two swindlers, showing and explaining the magnificent pattern, which, however, did not exist.

"I am not stupid," said the man. "It is therefore my high office for which I am not fit. But I must not let anyone know it;" and he praised the cloth, which he did not see, and expressed his joy at the beautiful colours and the fine pattern. "It is very excellent," he said later to the emperor.

Everybody in the whole town talked about the precious cloth.

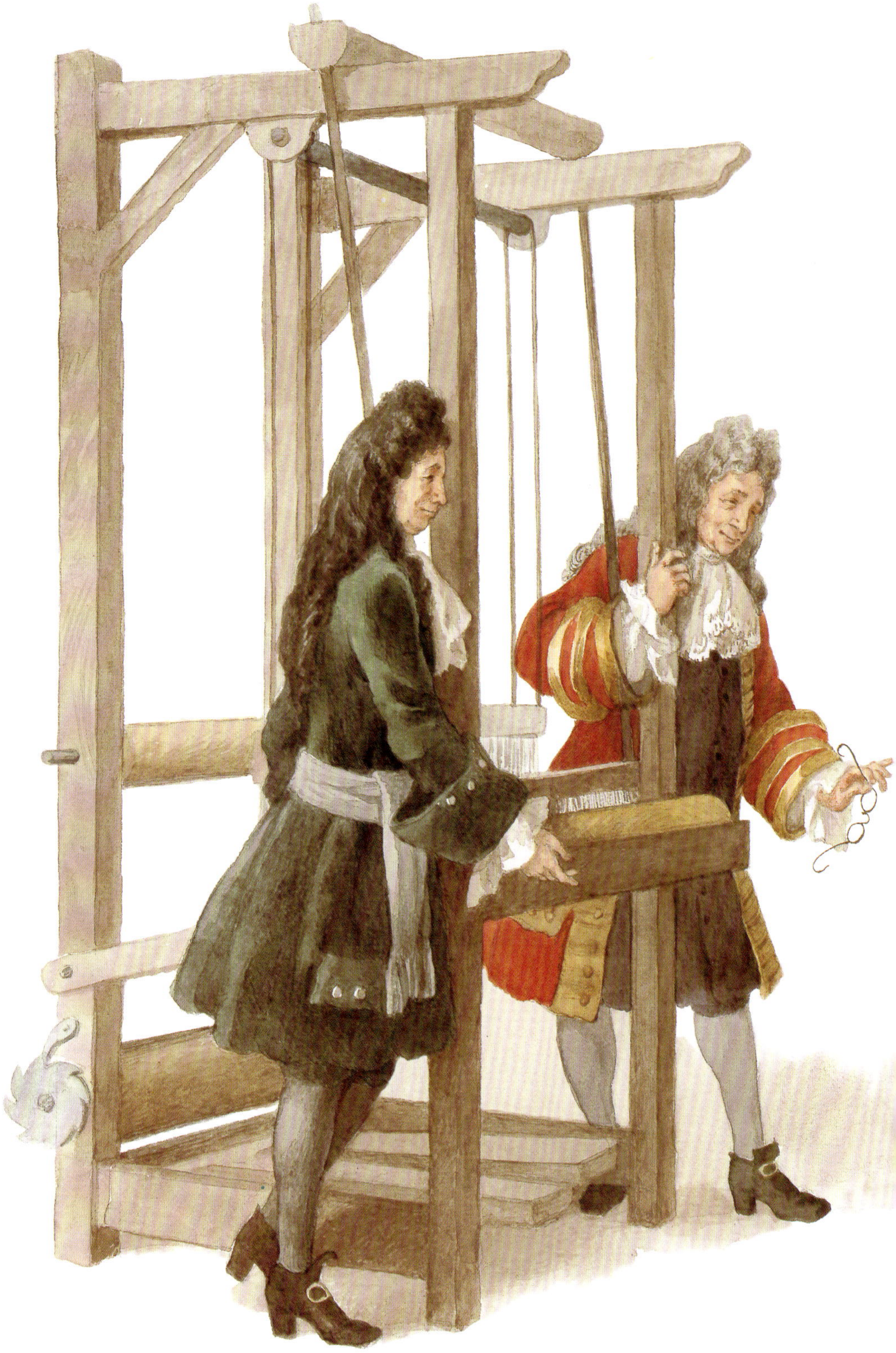

At last the emperor wished to see it himself, while it was still on the loom. With a number of courtiers, he went to the two clever swindlers, who now worked as hard as they could, but without using any thread.

"Is it not magnificent?" said the two old statesmen who had been there before. "Your Majesty must admire the colours and the pattern." And then they pointed to the empty looms, for they imagined the others could see the cloth.

"What is this?" thought the emperor, "I don't see anything at all. This is terrible! Am I stupid? Am I unfit to be emperor? That would indeed be the most dreadful thing that could happen to me."

"Really," he said, turning to the weavers, "your cloth has our most gracious approval." And nodding contentedly he looked at the empty loom, for he did not like to say that he saw nothing. All his attendants, who were with him, looked and looked, and although they could not see any more than the others, they said, like the emperor, "It is very beautiful." And all advised him to wear the new magnificent clothes at a great procession which was soon to take place. Everybody was delighted, and the emperor appointed the two swindlers "Imperial Court weavers."

The whole night previous to the day of the procession, the swindlers pretended to work, and burned more than sixteen candles. They pretended to take the cloth from the loom, and worked about in the air with big scissors, and sewed with needles without thread, and said at last: "The emperor's new suit is ready now."

The emperor then came to the hall; the swindlers held their arms up as if they held something in their hands and said: "These are the trousers!" "This is the coat!" and "Here is the cloak!" and so on. "They are all as light as a cobweb, and one feels as if one had nothing at all upon the body; but that is just the beauty of them."

"Indeed!" said all the courtiers; but they could not see anything.

"Does it please your Majesty now to undress," said the swindlers, "that we may assist your Majesty in putting on the new suit before the looking-glass?"

The emperor undressed, and the swindlers pretended to put the new suit upon him, one piece after another, while the emperor looked at himself in the glass from every side.

"How well they look! How well they fit!" said all. "What a beautiful pattern! What fine colours! That is a magnificent suit of clothes!"

Then it was announced that the bearers of the canopy for the procession were ready.

"I too am ready," said the emperor. "Doesn't my suit fit me marvellously?" Then he turned once more to the looking-glass, pretending to admire his garments.

The chamberlains who were to carry the train, stretched their hands to the ground as if they lifted up a train, and pretended to hold something in their hands. They did not like people to know that they couldn't see a thing.

Beneath the beautiful canopy the emperor set off to march in the procession, and all who saw him in the street exclaimed: "Indeed, the emperor's new suit is amazing! How well it fits him!"

Nobody wished to say they saw nothing, for then they would have been thought stupid or unfit for their office.

"But he has nothing on at all," said a little child at last.

"Heavens! listen to the voice of an innocent child," smiled the father, but one after another, more and more people whispered what the child had said. "But he has nothing on!," they all cried at last. That made a deep impression upon the emperor, for it seemed to him that they were right; but he thought to himself, "I must bear up to the end."

And the chamberlains walked with still greater dignity, carrying the long train which simply did not exist.

The Brave Tin Soldier

THERE were once five-and-twenty tin soldiers, all brothers, for they had been made out of the same old tin spoon. They shouldered arms and looked straight before them, and wore a splendid uniform, red and blue. The first thing in the world they ever heard were the words, "Tin soldiers!" uttered by a little boy, who clapped his hands with delight when the lid of the box, in which they lay, was taken off.

He stood at the table to set them up. The soldiers were all exactly alike, except one who had only one leg; he had been left to the last, and then there was not enough of the melted tin to finish him, so they made him to stand firmly on only one leg.

The table on which the tin soldiers stood, was covered with other playthings, but the most attractive to the eye was a pretty little paper castle.

Through the small windows the rooms could be seen. In front of the castle a number of little trees surrounded a piece of looking-glass, which was intended to represent a transparent lake. Swans, made of wax, swam on the lake, and were reflected in it.

All this was very pretty, but the prettiest of all was a tiny little lady, who stood at the open door of the castle.

She was made of paper, and she wore a dress of clear muslin, with a narrow blue ribbon over her shoulders just like a scarf. The little lady was a dancer, and she stretched out both her arms, and raised one of her legs so high, that the tin soldier thought that she, like himself, had only one leg.

"That is the wife for me," he thought; "but she is too grand, and lives in a castle, while I have only a box to live in, that is no place for her. Still I must try and make her acquaintance."

Then he laid himself at full length on the table behind a snuff-box so that he could peep at the little delicate lady, who continued to stand on one leg without losing her balance.

When evening came, the other tin soldiers were all placed in the box, and the people of the house went to bed. Then the toys began to play together, to pay visits, to have pretend fights. The tin soldiers rattled in their box; they wanted to get out and join the fun, but they could not open the lid. The nut-crackers played at leap-frog, and the pencil jumped about the table. There was such a noise that the canary woke up and began to sing. Only the tin soldier and the dancer remained in their places. She stood on tiptoe, with her legs stretched out, as firmly as he did on his one leg. He never took his eyes from her for even a moment. Then, just as the clock struck twelve, the lid of the snuff-box sprang open; but, instead of snuff, there jumped up a little black goblin.

"Tin soldier," said the goblin, "don't wish for what does not belong to you." But the tin soldier pretended not to hear.

"Wait till tomorrow, then," said the goblin.

When the children came in the next morning, they placed the tin soldier in the window. Now, whether it was the goblin who did it, or the draught, is not known, but the window flew open, and out fell the tin soldier, heels over head, from the third story, into the street beneath. It was a terrible fall; for he came head downwards, his helmet and his bayonet stuck in between the flagstones, and his one leg up in the air. The servant maid and the little boy went down stairs directly to look for him; but he was nowhere to be seen.

If he had called out, "Here I am," it would have been all right, but he was too proud to cry out for help while he wore a uniform.

Presently it began to rain, and the drops fell faster and faster, till there was a heavy shower. When it was over, two boys happened to pass by, and one of them said, "Look, there is a tin soldier. He ought to have a boat to sail in."

So they made a boat out of a newspaper, and placed the tin soldier in it, and sent him sailing down the gutter, while the two boys ran by the side of it, and clapped their hands. Good gracious, what large waves arose in that gutter! and how fast the stream rolled on! for the rain had been very heavy. The paper boat rocked up and down, and turned itself round sometimes so quickly that the tin soldier trembled; yet he remained firm; his countenance did not change; he looked straight before him, and shouldered his musket. Suddenly the boat shot under a bridge which formed a part of a drain, and then it was as dark as the tin soldier's box.

"Where am I going now?" thought he. "This is the black goblin's fault, I am sure. Ah, well, if the little lady were only here with me in the boat, I should not care for any darkness."

Suddenly there appeared a great water-rat, who lived in the drain.

"Have you a passport?" asked the rat, "give it to me at once." But the tin soldier remained silent and held his musket tighter than ever. The boat sailed on and the rat followed it. How he did gnash his teeth and cry out to the bits of wood and straw, "Stop him, stop him; he has not paid toll, and has not shown his pass." But the stream rushed on stronger and stronger. The tin soldier could already see daylight shining where the arch ended. Then he heard a roaring sound quite terrible enough to frighten the bravest man. At the end of the tunnel the drain fell into a large canal over a steep place, which made it as dangerous for him as a waterfall would be to us. He was too near to it to stop, so the boat rushed on, and the poor tin soldier could only hold himself as stiffly as possible, without moving an eyelid, to show that he was not afraid.

The boat whirled round three or four times, and then filled with water to the very edge; nothing could save it from sinking. He now stood up to his neck in water, while the boat sank deeper and deeper, and the paper became soft and loose with the wet, till at last the water closed over the soldier's head. He thought of the elegant little dancer whom he should never see again, and the words of the song sounded in his ears:

"Farewell, warrior! ever brave,
Drifting onward to thy grave."

Then the paper boat fell to pieces, and the soldier sank into the water and immediately afterwards was swallowed up by a great fish. Oh, how dark it was inside the fish! A great deal darker than in the tunnel, and narrower too, but the tin soldier continued firm, and lay at full length shouldering his musket.

The fish swam to and fro, making the most wonderful movements, but at last he became quite still. After a while, a flash of lightning seemed to pass through him, and then daylight shone and a voice cried out, "I declare here is the tin soldier." The fish had been caught, taken to the market and sold to the cook, who took him into the kitchen and was now cutting him open with a large knife.

Picking up the soldier between her finger and thumb, the cook carried him into the room. They were all anxious to see this wonderful soldier who had travelled about inside a fish; but he was not at all proud. They placed him on the table, and — how many curious things do happen in the world! — there he was in the very same room from the window of which he had fallen, there were the same children, the same toys on the table, and the pretty castle with the elegant little dancer at the door. She still balanced herself on one leg, and held up the other, so she was as firm as himself. It touched the tin soldier so much to see her that he almost wept tin tears, but he kept them back. He only looked at her and they both remained silent.

Presently one of the little boys took up the tin soldier, and threw him into the stove. He had no reason for doing so, therefore it must have been the fault of the black goblin who lived in the snuff-box. The flames lighted up the tin soldier, as he stood, the heat was very terrible, but whether it proceeded from the real fire or from the fire of love he could not tell. Then he could see that the bright colours were faded from his uniform, but whether they had been washed off during his journey or from the effects of his sorrow, no one could say. He looked at the little lady, and she looked at him. He felt himself melting away, but he still remained firm with his gun on his shoulder. Suddenly the door of the room flew open and the draught of air caught up the little dancer. She fluttered like a sylph right into the stove by the side of the tin soldier, and was instantly in flames and was gone.

The tin soldier melted down into a lump, and the next morning, when the maid servant took the ashes out of the stove, she found him in the shape of a little tin heart. But of the little dancer nothing remained but the tinsel rose, which was burnt black as a cinder.

The Little Match-Seller

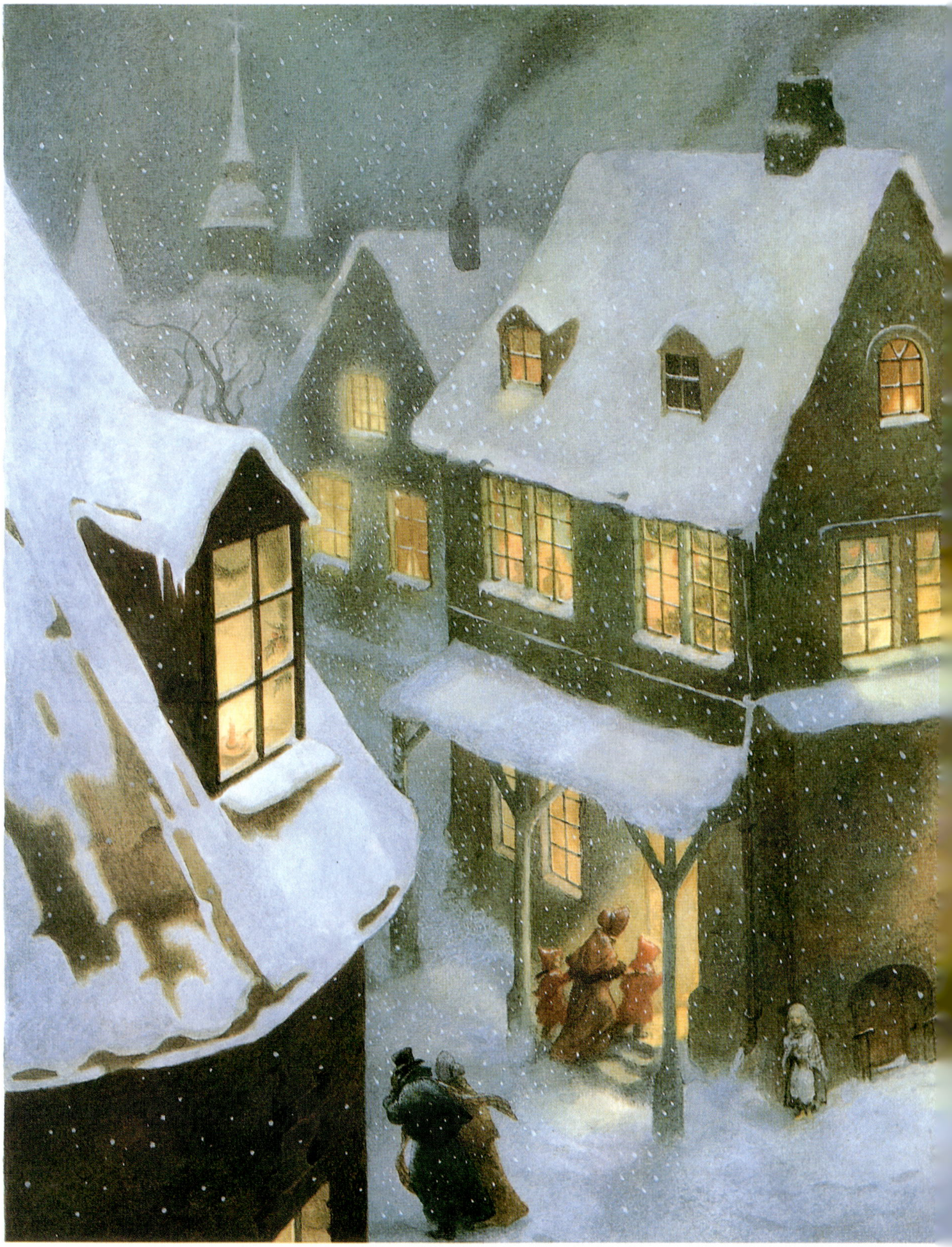

IT was terribly cold and nearly dark on the last evening of the old year, and the snow was falling fast.

In the cold and the darkness, a poor little girl, with bare head and naked feet, roamed through the streets. The poor little creature had lost her shoes in running across the street to avoid a carriage. So the little girl walked on with her tiny feet quite red and blue with the cold. In an old apron she carried a number of matches, and had a bundle of them in her hands. No one had bought anything from her the whole day, nor had anyone given her even a penny.

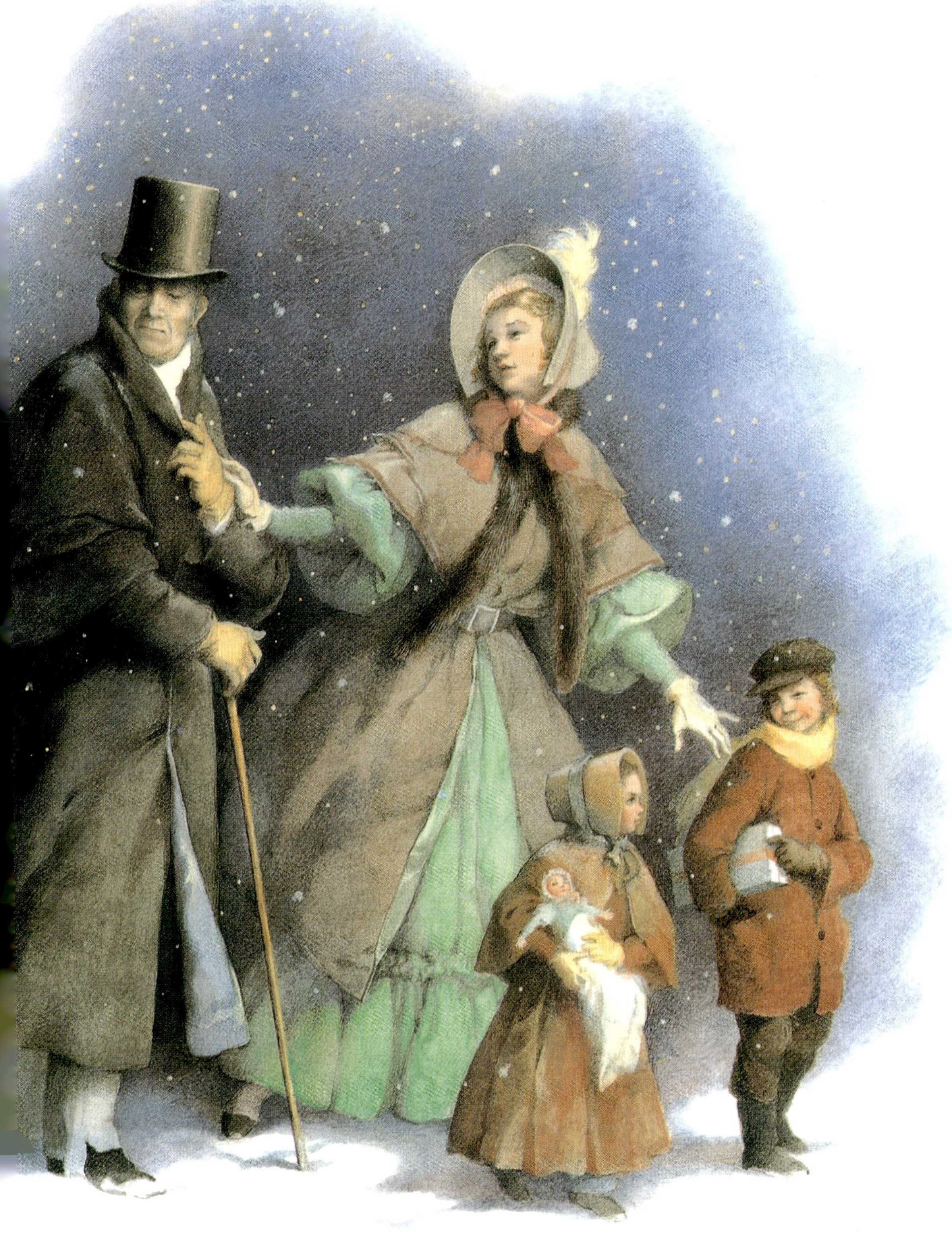

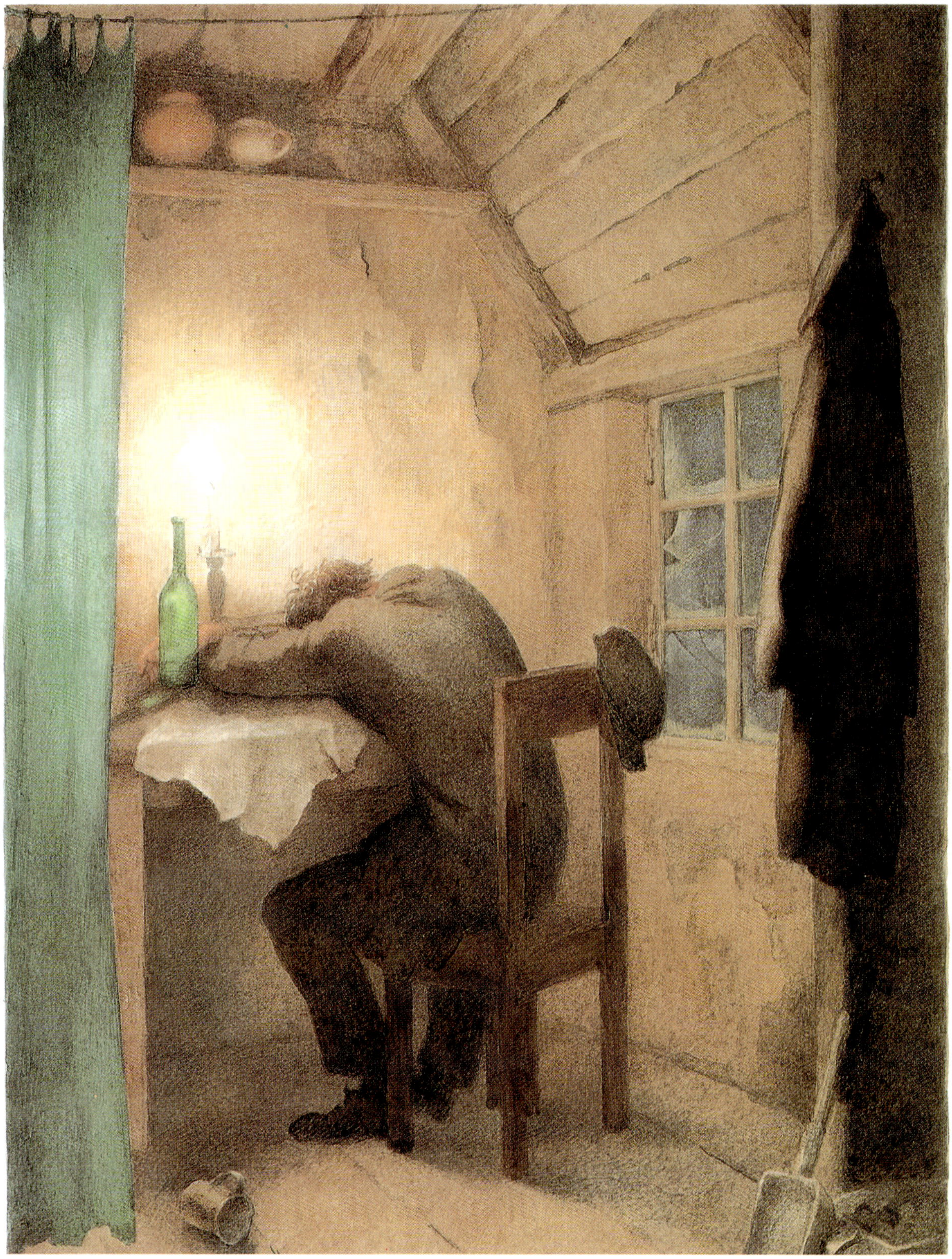

Shivering with cold and hunger, she crept along. Poor little child, she looked the picture of misery. The snowflakes fell on her long, fair hair, which hung in curls on her shoulders.

In a corner, between two houses, one of which projected beyond the other, she sank down and huddled herself together. She dared not go home without even a penny. Her father would certainly beat her. Her little hands were almost frozen with the cold. Ah! perhaps a burning match might be some good, if she could draw it from the bundle and strike it against the wall, just to warm her fingers. She drew one out — "scratch!" how it sputtered as it burnt! It gave a warm, bright light, like a little candle.

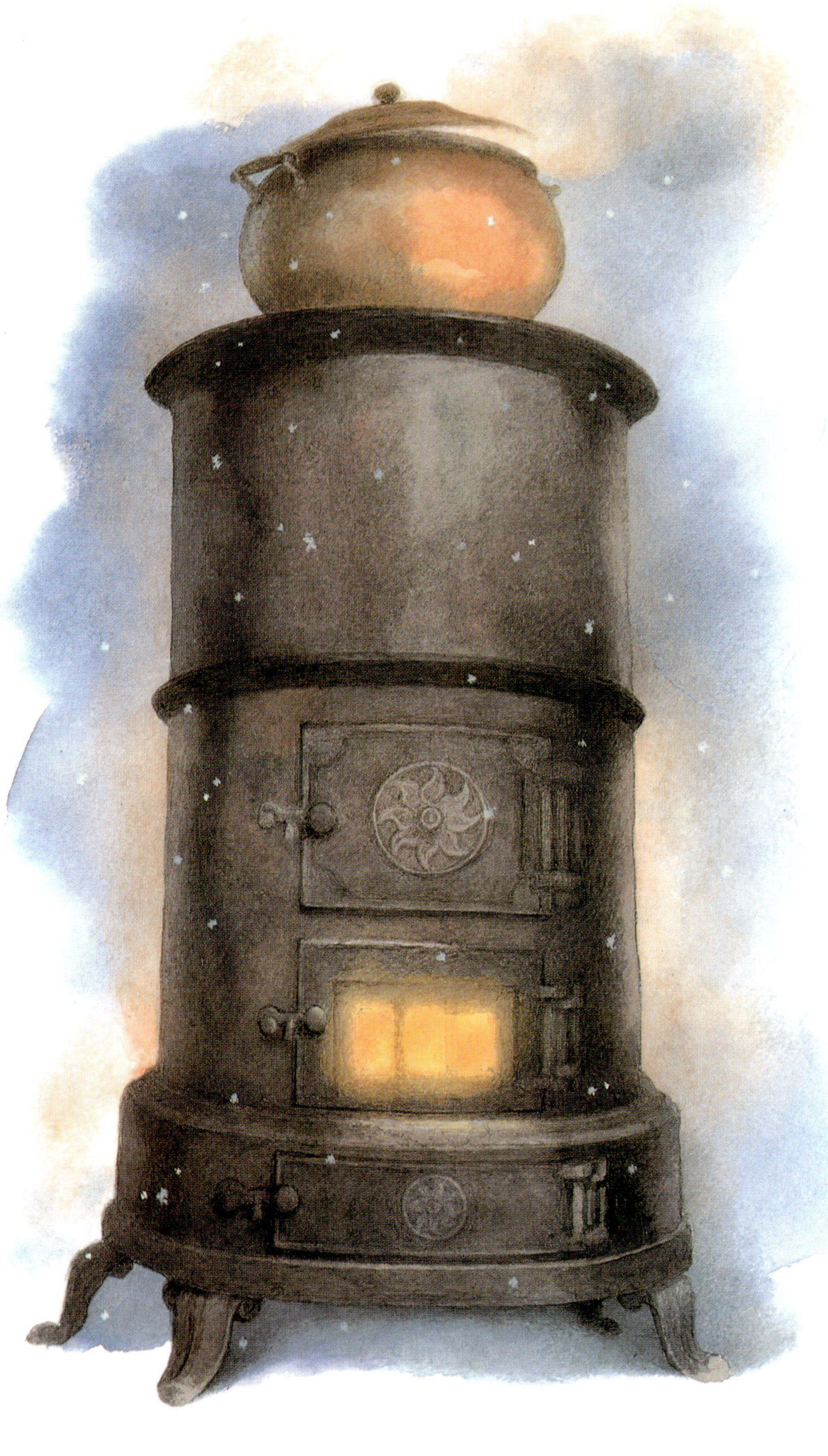

The match gave a wonderful light. It seemed to the little girl that she was sitting by a large iron stove, with polished brass feet and a brass ornament. The fire seemed so beautifully warm that the child stretched out her feet as if to warm them. Then suddenly the flame went out, the stove vanished, and she had only the remains of the half-burnt match in her hand.

She rubbed another match on the wall. It burst into a flame, and where its light fell upon the wall it became as transparent as a veil, and she could see into the room. The table was covered with a snowy white table-cloth, on which stood a splendid dinner service, and a steaming roast goose, stuffed with apples and dried plums. And what was still more wonderful, the goose jumped down from the dish and waddled across the floor, with a knife and fork in its breast, towards the little girl. Then the match went out, and there remained nothing but the thick, damp, cold wall before her.

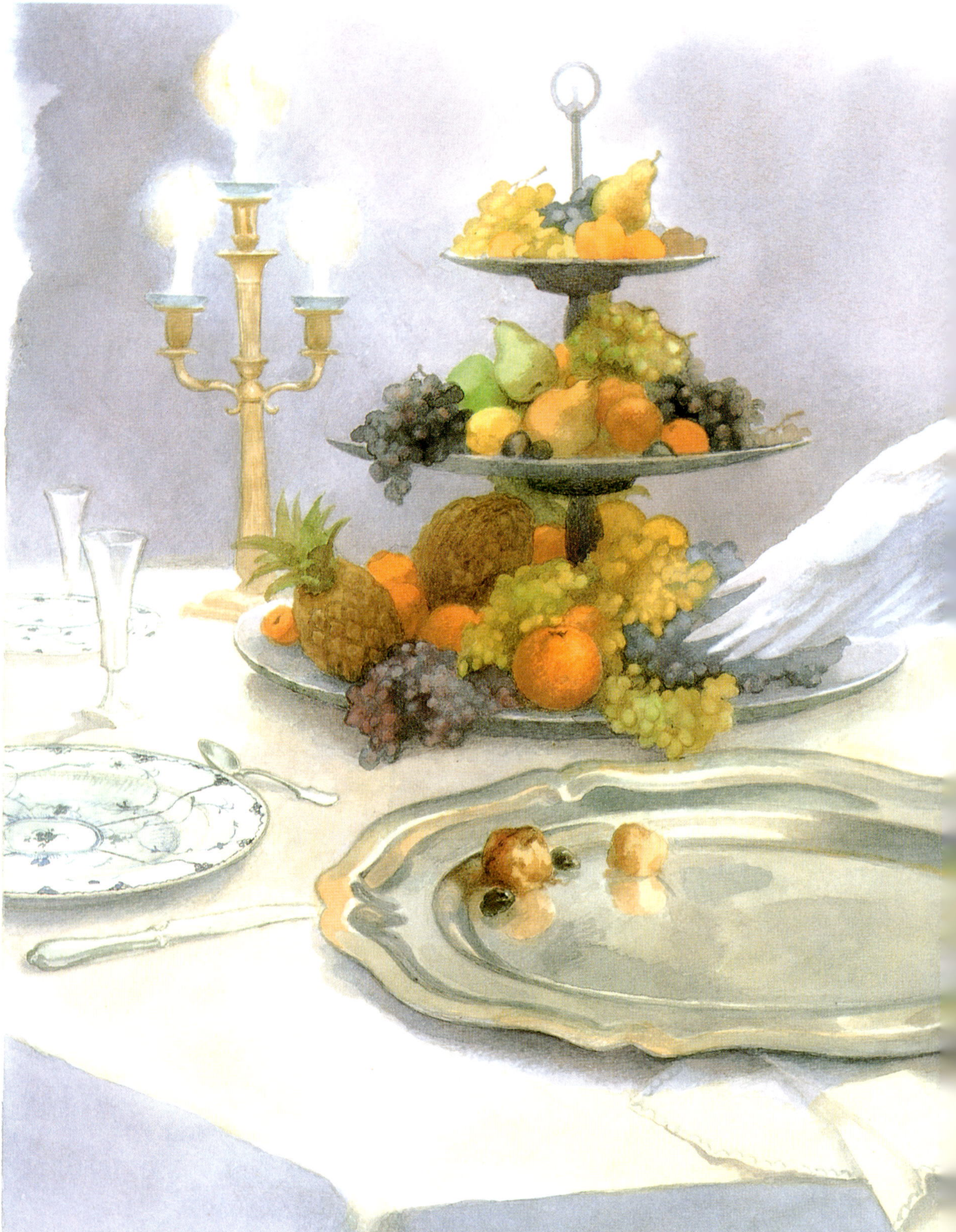

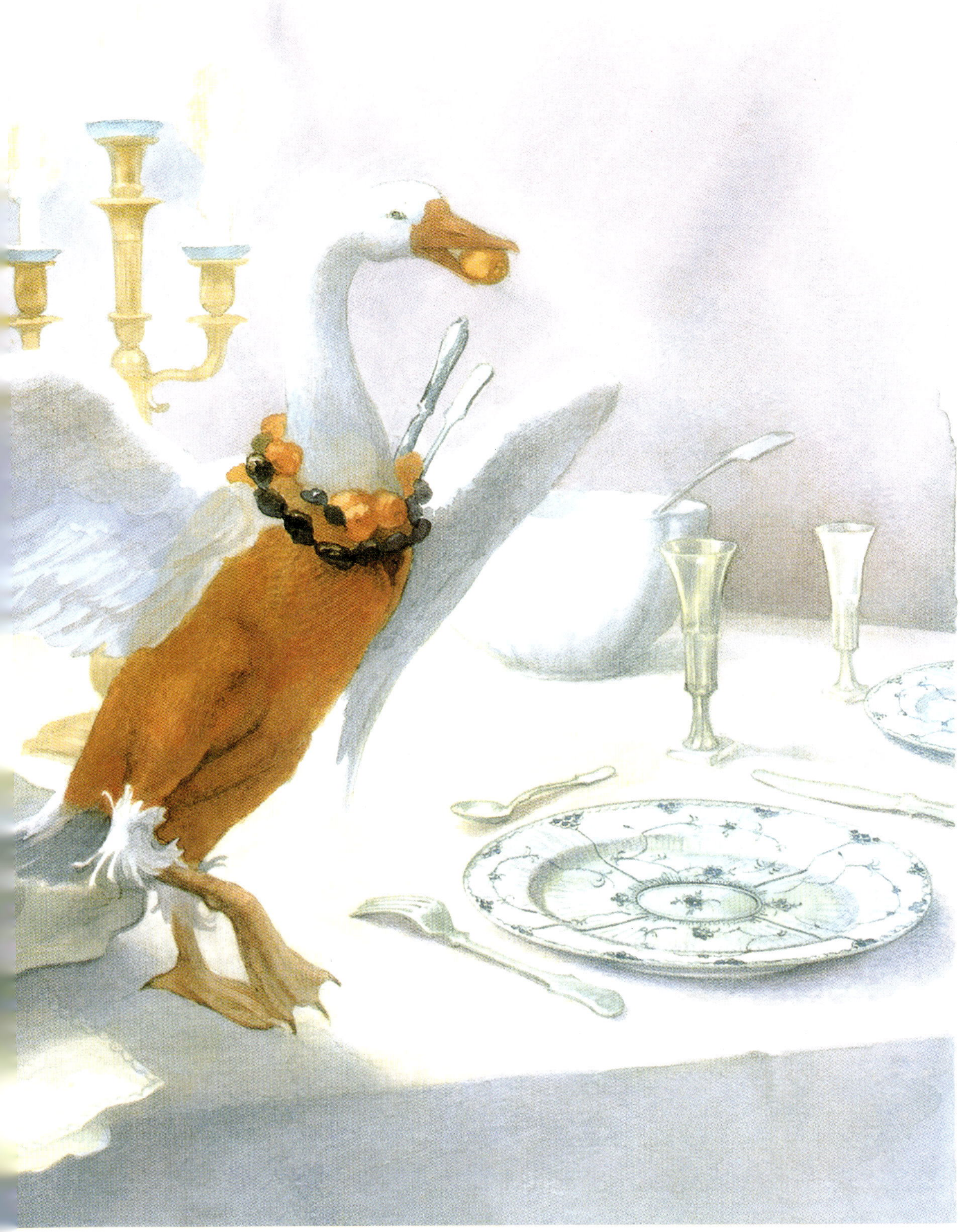

She lighted another match, and then she found herself sitting under a beautiful Christmas-tree. Candles were burning upon the green branches, and coloured ribbons like those she had seen in the shop-windows, stretched from side to side. The little one stretched out her hand towards them, and the match went out.

The Christmas lights rose higher and higher, till they looked to her like the stars in the sky. Then she saw a star fall, leaving behind it a bright streak of fire. "Someone is dying," thought the little girl, for her old grandmother, the only one who had ever loved her, and who was now dead, had told her that when a star falls, a soul was going up to God.

She again rubbed a match on the wall, and the light shone round her; in the brightness stood her old grandmother, clear and shining, yet mild and loving in her appearance.

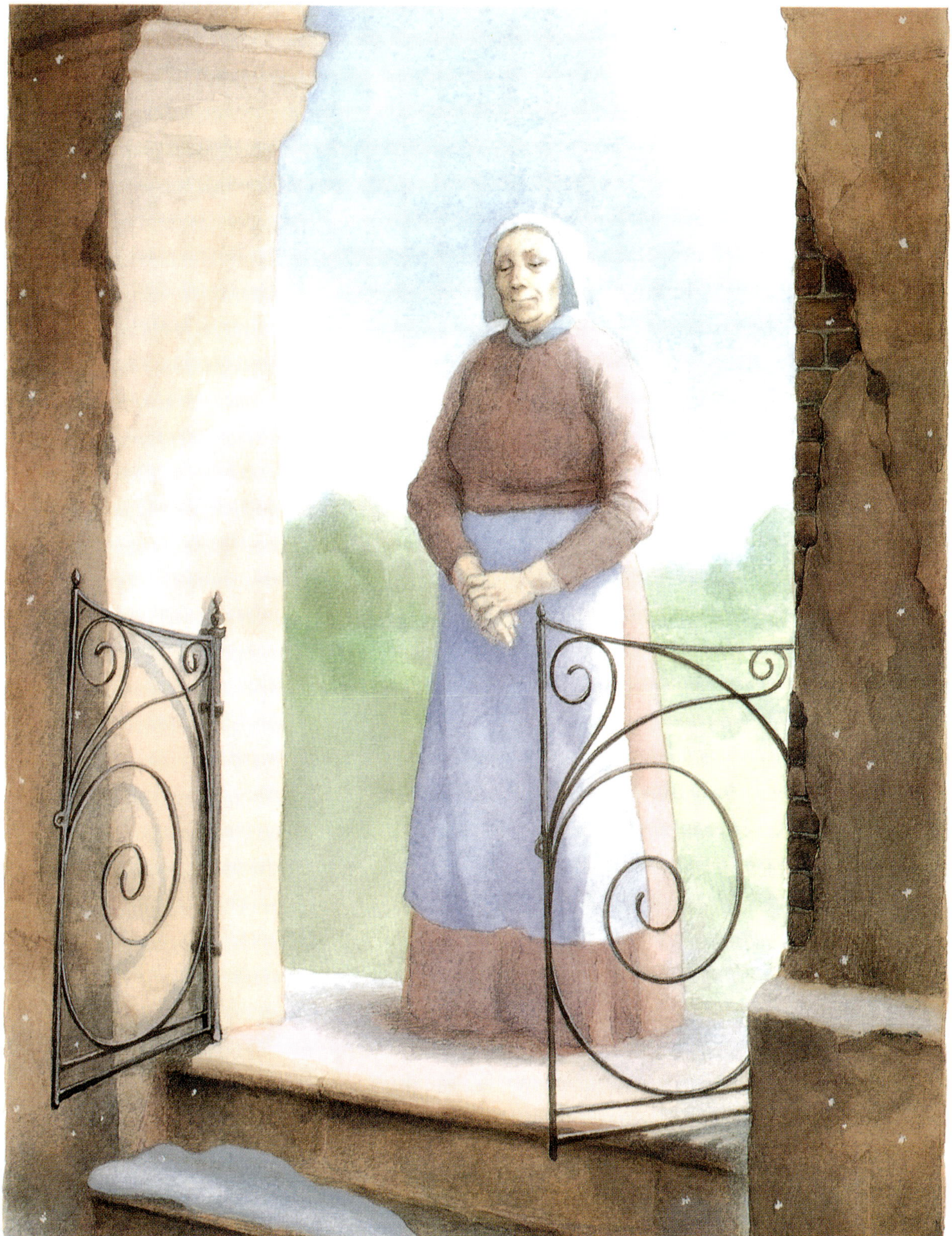

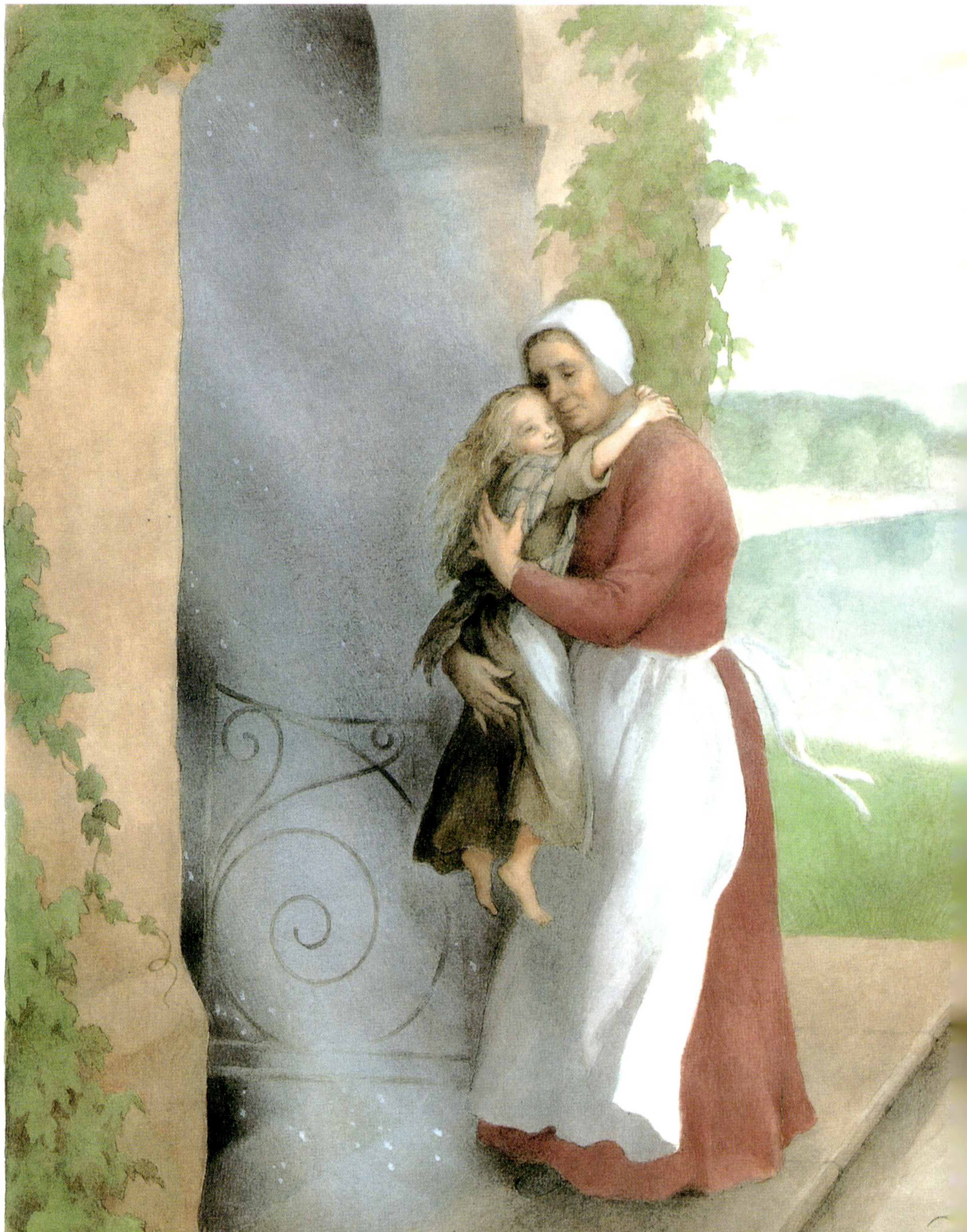

"Grandmother," cried the little one, "O take me with you. Don't vanish away when the match burns out." She made haste to light the whole bundle of matches, for she wished to keep her grandmother there. The matches glowed with a light that was brighter than the noon-day, and her grandmother took the little girl in her arms.

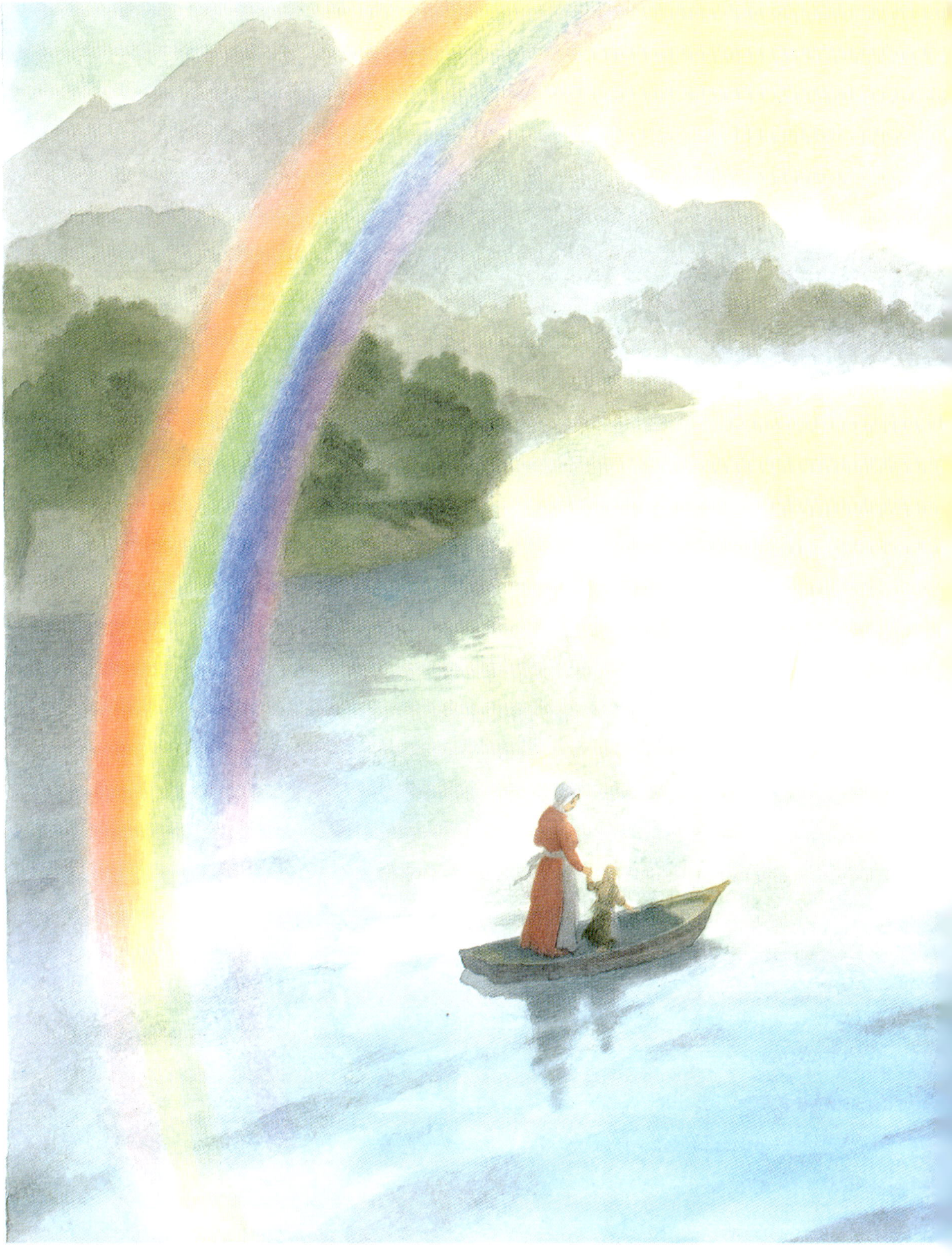

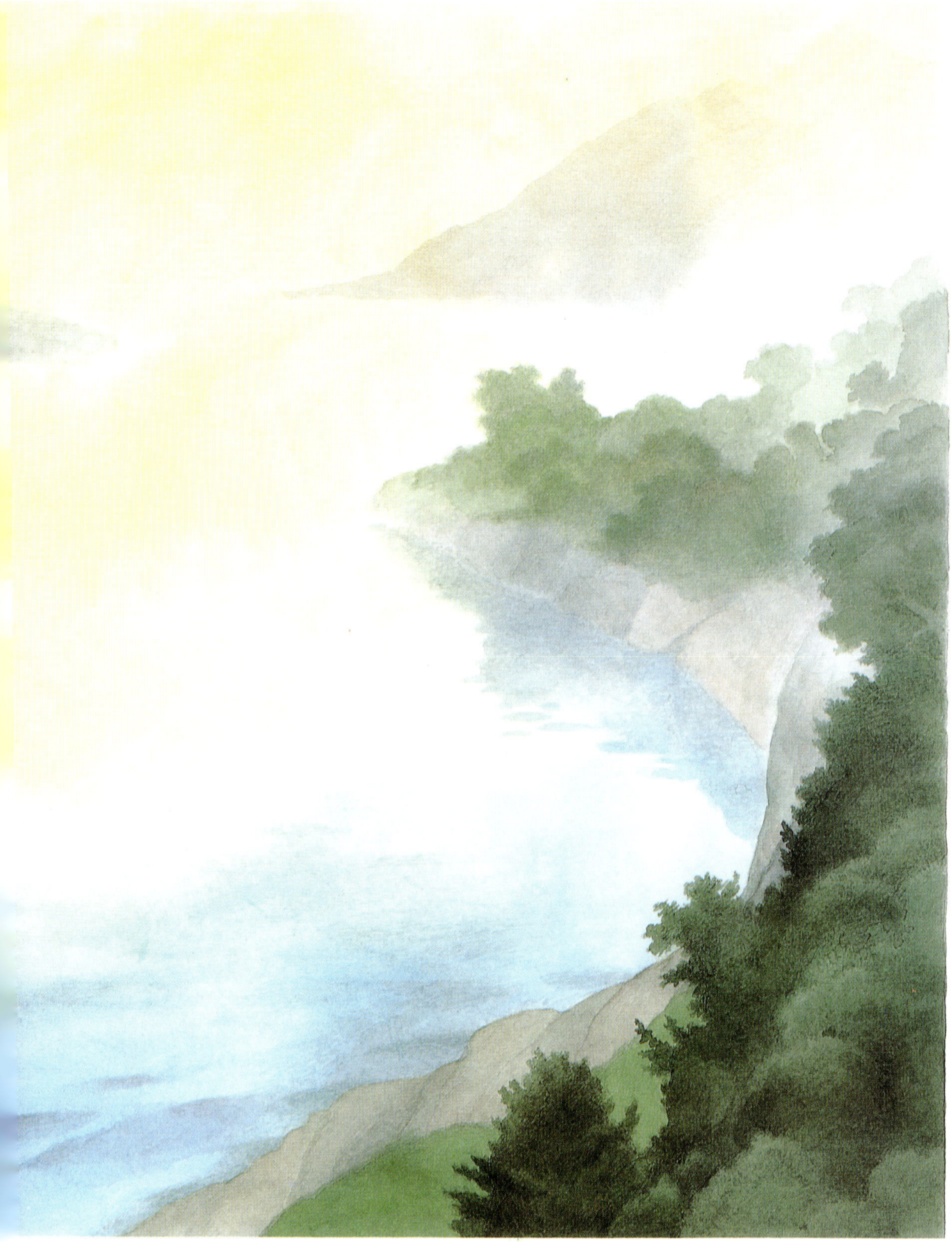

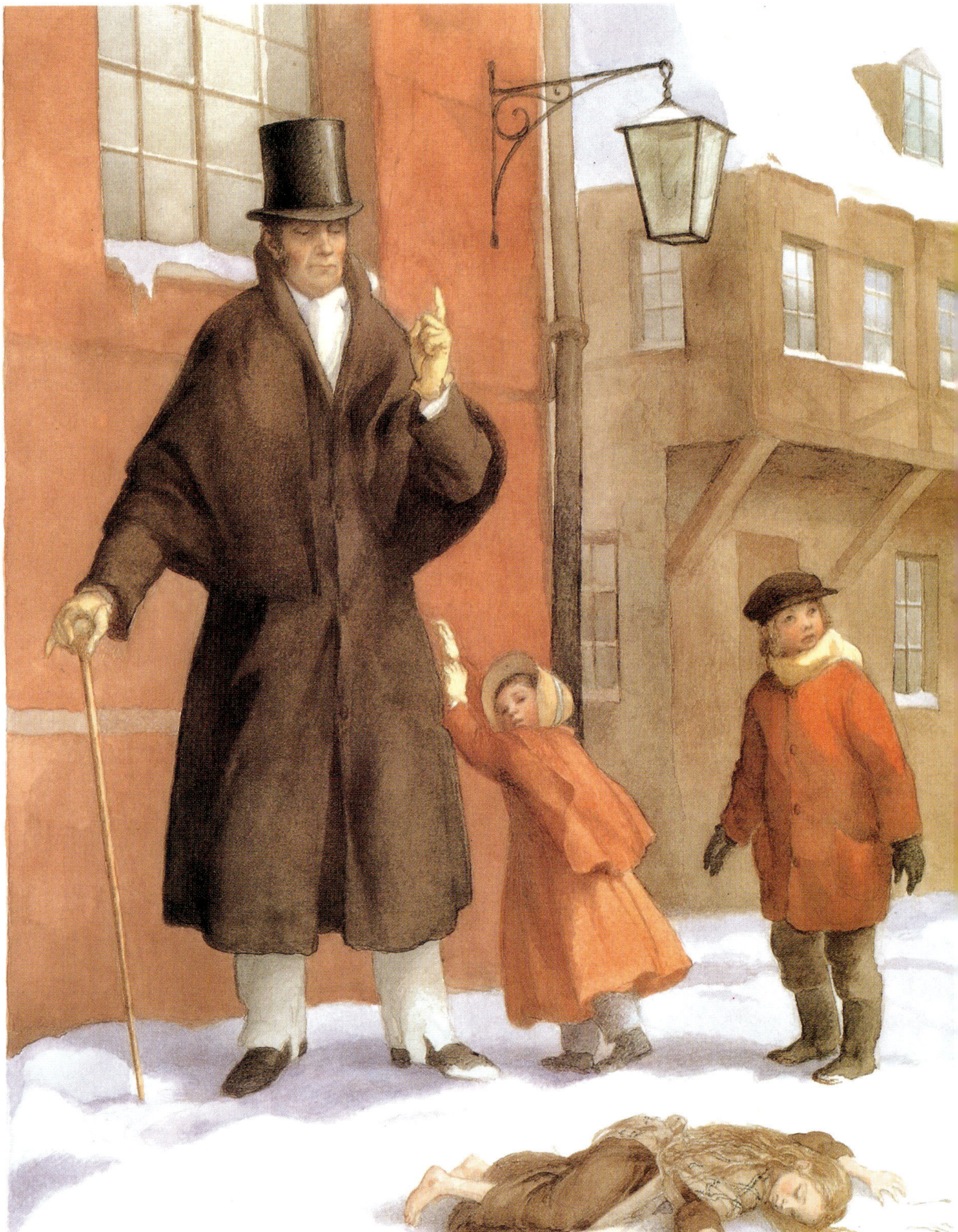

They both flew upwards in brightness and joy far above the earth, where there was neither cold nor hunger nor pain, for they were with God.

In the morning there in the street lay the poor little one, with pale cheeks and smiling mouth. She had frozen to death. In the stiffness of death, she still held the burnt matches in her hand. "She tried to warm herself," said some.

No one imagined what beautiful things she had seen, nor into what glory she had entered with her grandmother that day.

The Little Mermaid

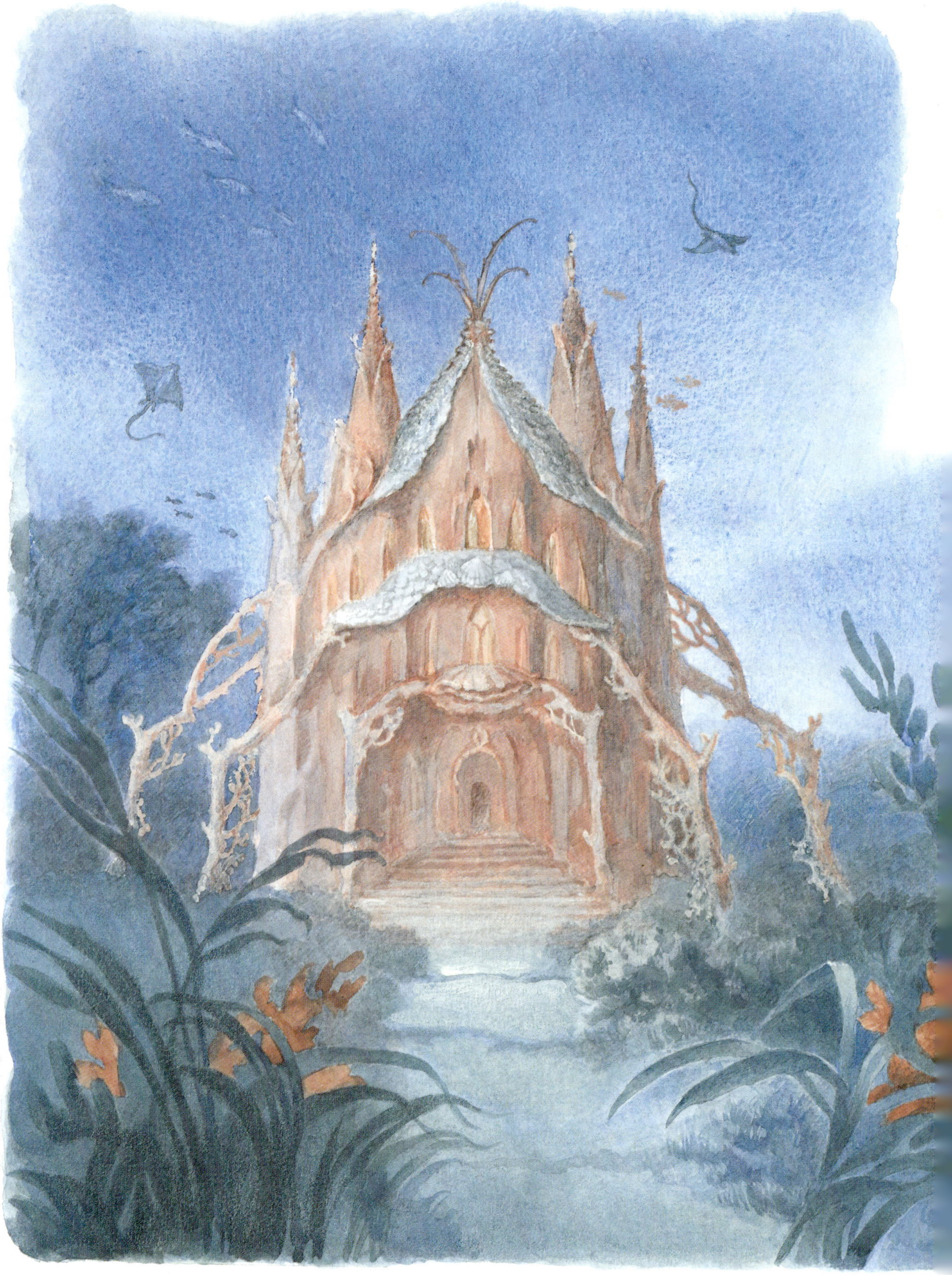

FAR out in the ocean, where the water is as blue as the prettiest cornflower and as clear as crystal, it is very, very deep. In the deepest spot of all, stands the castle of the Sea King. The roof is formed of shells that open and close as the water flows over them, and in each lies a glittering pearl.

The Sea King's wife had died and his aged mother kept house for him. She was a wise woman, and cared especially for the little sea-princesses, her six grand-daughters. The youngest was the prettiest of them all; her skin was as delicate as a rose-leaf, and her eyes as blue as the deepest sea.

All day long they played in the great halls of the castle, or among the living flowers of the sea. The fish swam up and ate out of their hands, and allowed themselves to be stroked.

Outside the castle there was a beautiful garden, in which grew bright red and dark blue flowers, and blossoms like flames of fire; the fruit glittered like gold, and the leaves and stems waved to and fro continually. Each of the young princesses had a little plot of ground, and in her garden the youngest grew flowers as red as sunset.

Other than her pretty red flowers, she cared for nothing except a beautiful marble statue of a handsome boy. It had fallen to the bottom of the sea from a wreck. She planted by the statue a rose-coloured weeping willow. It grew splendidly, and very soon hung its fresh branches over the statue, almost down to the blue sands.

Nothing gave the little mermaid so much pleasure as to hear about the world above the sea. She made her old grandmother tell her all she knew of the ships and of the towns, the people and the animals.

"When you have reached your fifteenth year," said the grandmother, "you will be allowed to swim up and sit on the rocks in the moonlight, while the great ships are sailing by."

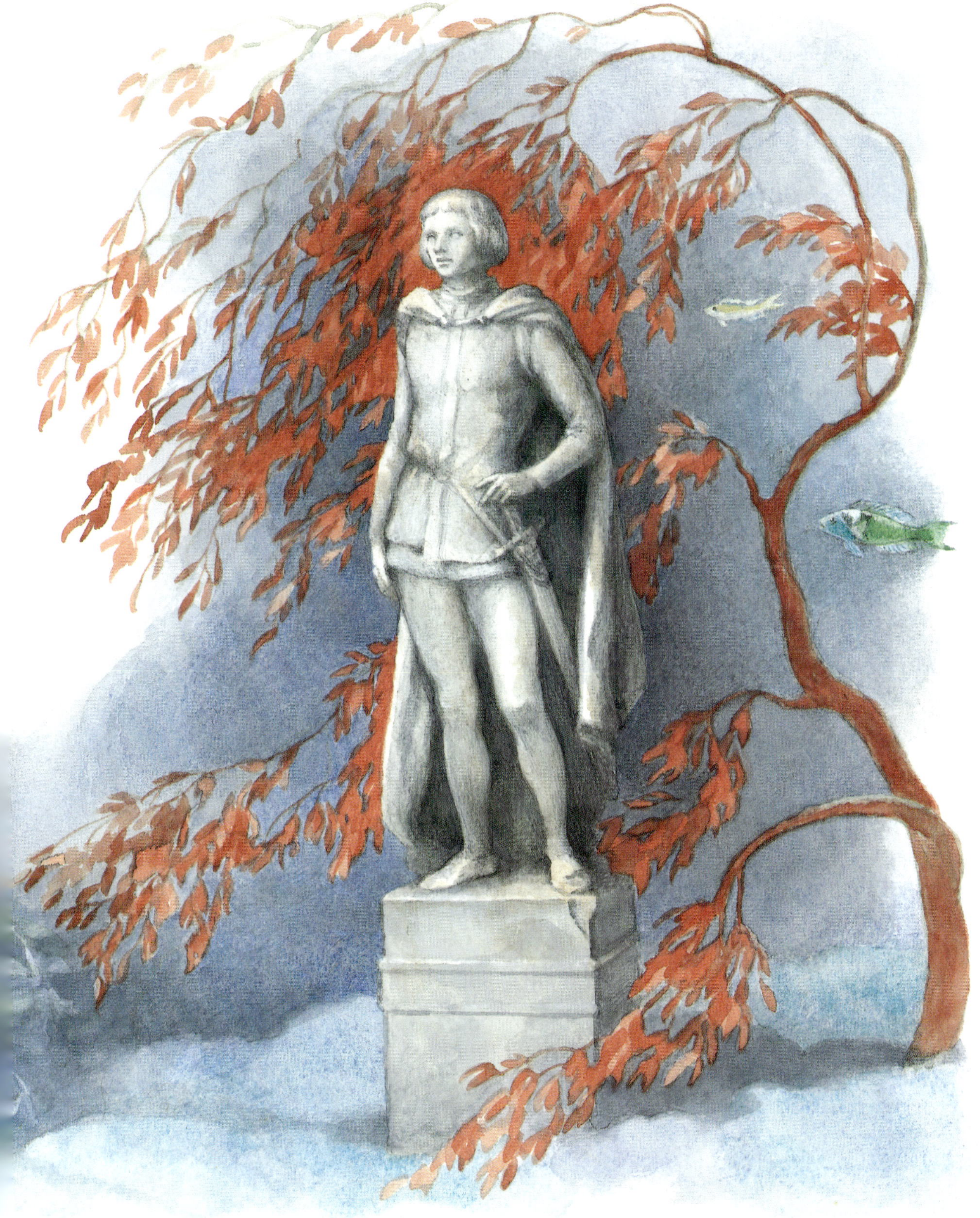

Many nights the youngest princess stood by the open window, looking up through the dark blue water, and watching the fish as they splashed about with their fins and tails. She could see the moon and stars shining faintly; but through the water they looked larger than they do to our eyes.

As soon as the eldest was fifteen, she was allowed to rise to the surface of the ocean. When she came back, she had hundreds of things to talk about;

but the most beautiful, she said, was to lie in the moonlight, on a sandbank, in the quiet sea, near the coast, and to gaze on a large town nearby, where the lights were twinkling like hundreds of stars.

Afterwards, when the youngest princess stood at the open window looking up through the dark blue water, she thought of the great city, with all its bustle and noise, and even fancied she could hear the sound of the church bells, down in the depths of the sea.

In another year the second sister was allowed to swim to the surface of the water. She arrived just as the sun was setting, and this, she said, was the most beautiful sight of all.

The third sister's turn followed; she was the boldest of them all, and she swam up a broad river that emptied itself into the sea. There she found a whole troop of little human children sporting about in the water, even though they had not fish's tails.

The fourth sister was more timid; she remained in the midst of the sea, but she said it was quite as beautiful there. She could see for so many miles around her, and the sky above looked like a bell of glass.

The fifth sister's birthday occurred in the winter; so when her turn came, she saw what the others had not seen the first time they went up. The sea looked quite green, and large icebergs were floating about, of the most singular shapes, glittering like diamonds.

At last the youngest mermaid reached her fifteenth year. "Well, now, you are grown up," said her old grandmother, and she placed a wreath of white lilies in her hair.

Then the little princess said, "Farewell," and rose as lightly as a bubble to the surface of the water. The sea was calm, and the air mild and fresh. A large ship, with three masts, lay becalmed on the water, for not a breeze stirred. There was music and song on board; and, as darkness came on, a hundred coloured lanterns were lighted, as if the flags of all nations waved in the air.

The little mermaid swam close, and now and then, as the waves lifted her up, she could look in through clear glass window-panes, and see a number of well-dressed people within.

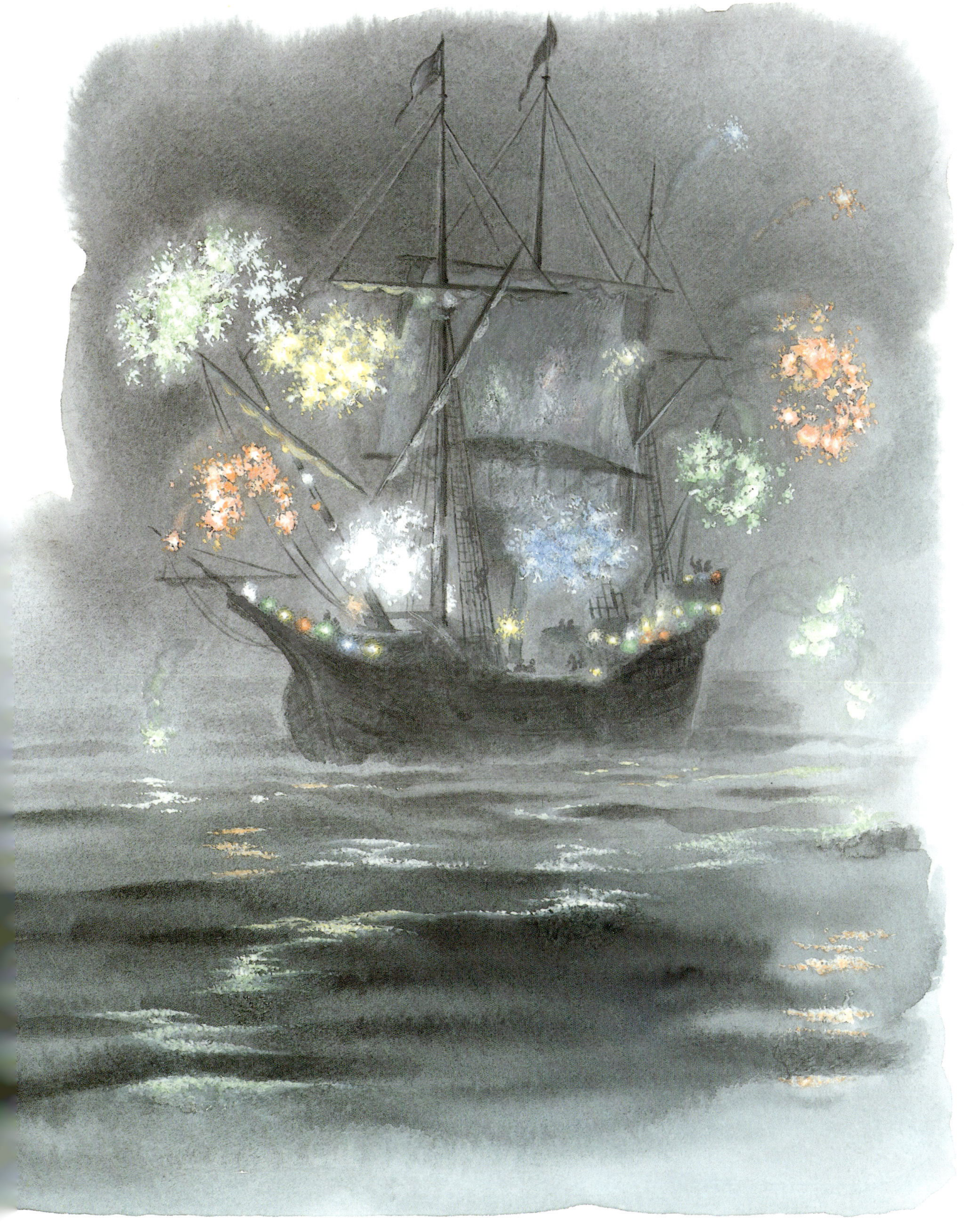

Through the glass she saw a young prince, the most beautiful of all, with large black eyes; he was sixteen years of age, and his birthday was being kept with much rejoicing.

The sailors were dancing on deck, but when the prince came out of the cabin, more than a hundred rockets rose in the air, making it as bright as day. The little mermaid had never seen such fireworks before. It appeared as if all the stars of heaven were falling around her. And how handsome the young prince looked, as he smiled at all those present, while the music resounded through the clear night air. She could not take her eyes from the ship, or from the beautiful prince.

After a while the noble ship continued her passage; but soon the waves rose higher and heavy clouds darkened the sky. A dreadful storm was approaching. The waves rose mountains high, and before long the ship gave way under the lashing of the sea as it broke over the deck; the mainmast snapped like a reed; the ship lay over on her side; and the water rushed in.

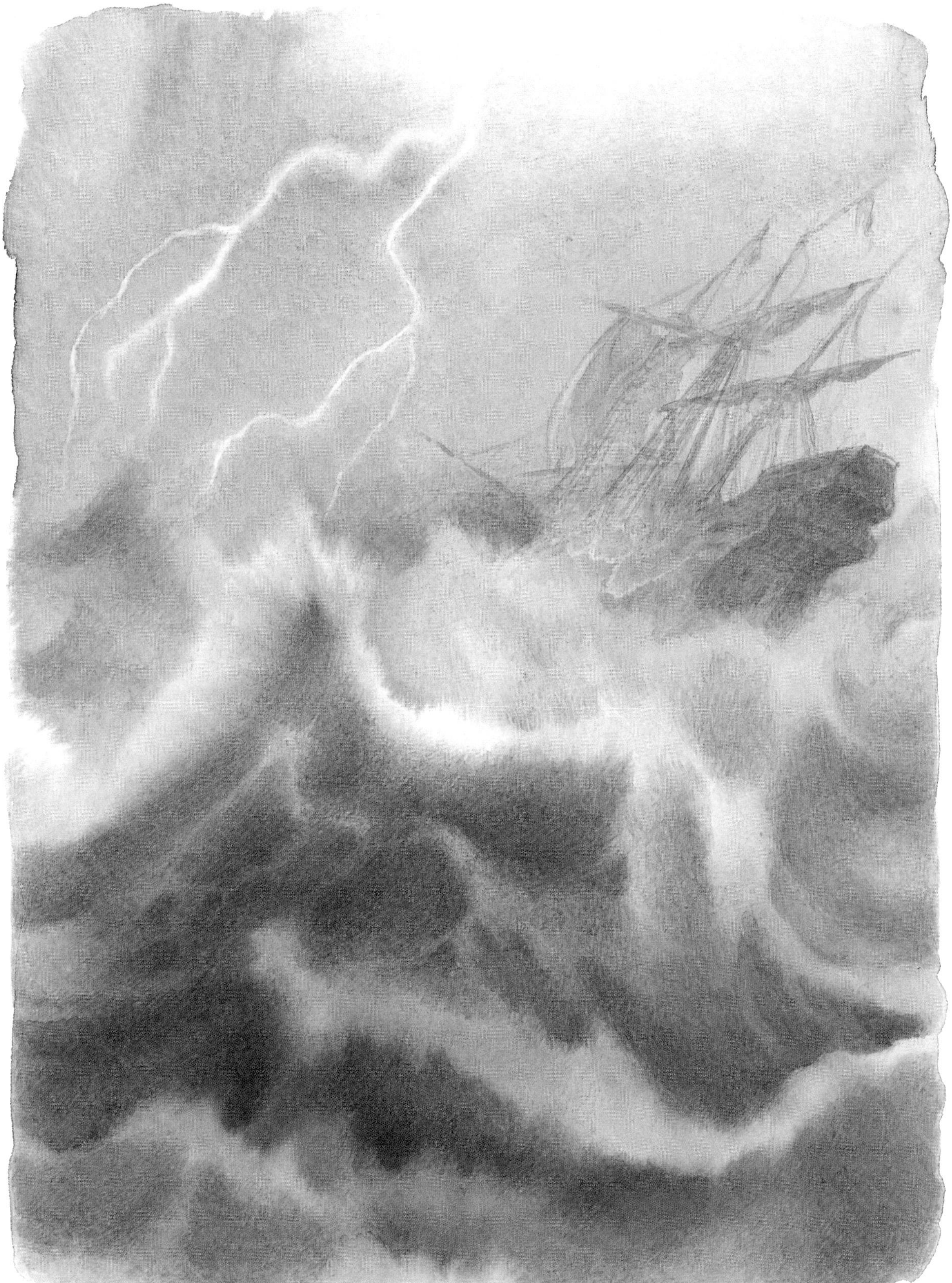

Seeing that the crew were in danger, the mermaid dived under the dark waters, rising and falling with the waves, till she managed to reach the young prince, who was fast losing strength in that stormy sea. His limbs were failing him, his beautiful eyes were closed, and he would have drowned had not the little mermaid come to his assistance. She held his head above the water, and let the waves carry them where they would.

Soon they came in sight of land.

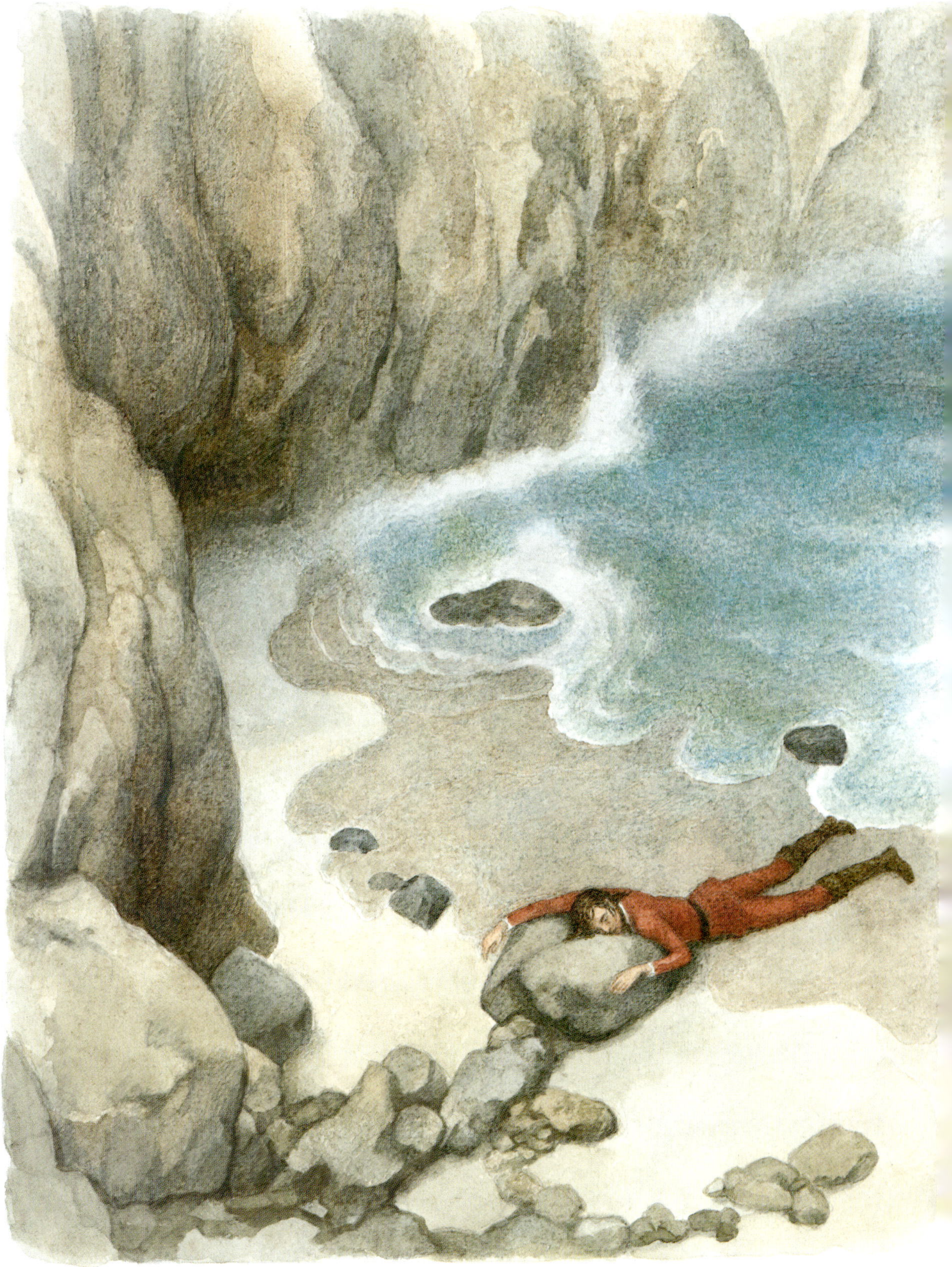

Near the coast stood a large white church or convent. The sea here formed a little bay, so she swam with the handsome prince to the beach, which was covered with fine, white sand, and there she laid him in the warm sunshine. Then bells sounded in the large white building, and a number of young girls came into the garden. The little mermaid swam out farther from the shore and watched to see what would become of the poor prince.

She did not wait long before she saw a young girl approach the spot where he lay. She seemed frightened at first, but only for a moment; then she fetched a number of people, and the mermaid saw that the prince came to life again, and smiled upon those who stood round him. But to her he sent no smile; he knew not that she had saved him. This made her very unhappy, and when he was led away into the great building, she dived down sorrowfully into the water, and returned to her father's castle.

Many an evening and morning she swam to the little bay but she never saw the prince and returned home, always more sorrowful than before. At length she could bear it no longer, and told her sisters all about it. Very soon it became known to two mermaids who happened to know where the prince came from, and where his palace stood.

"Come, little sister," said the other princesses; then they entwined their arms and rose up in a long row to the surface of the water, close by the spot where they knew the prince's palace stood. It was built of bright yellow stone, with long flights of marble steps, one of which reached right down to the sea. Gilded cupolas rose over the roof.

Now that she knew where he lived, the youngest princess spent many an evening and many a night on the water near the palace.

She started to swim closer and closer to the shore. One night she went right up the channel towards a marble balcony overlooking the water. Here she stayed and watched the young prince, who thought himself quite alone in the bright moonlight. She was glad she had saved his life when he had been tossed about half-dead on the waves, and she remembered how his head had rested on her bosom. But he knew nothing of all this.

She grew more and more fond of human beings, and wished more and more to wander in that upper world of theirs that seemed so much larger than her own.

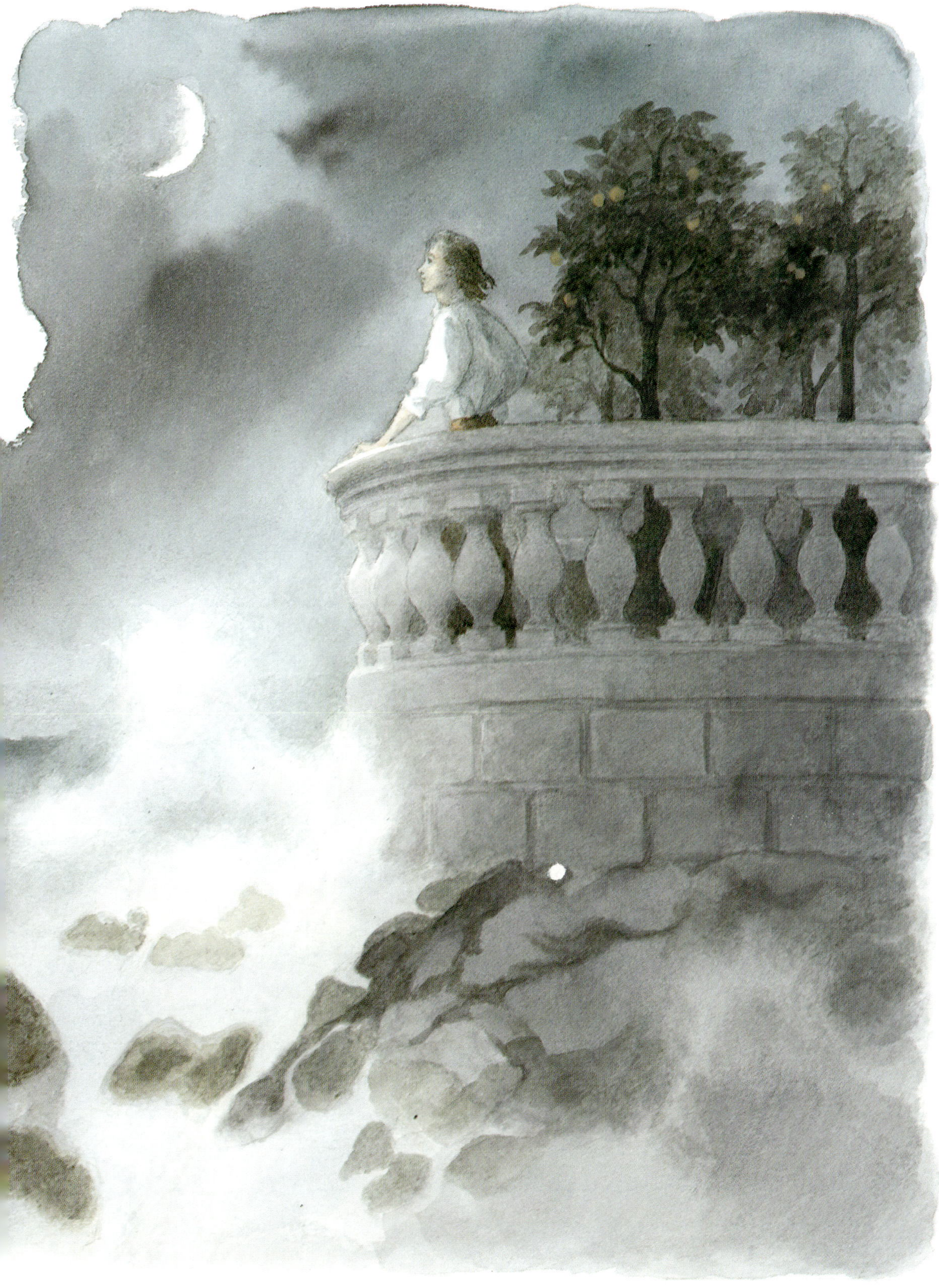

There was so much that she wished to know, she went to her old grandmother, who knew all about the lands above the sea.

"If human beings are not drowned," asked the little mermaid, "can they live forever? Do they never die as we do here in the sea?"

"Yes," replied the old lady, "they must also die, and their life is even shorter than ours. We sometimes live to three hundred years, but when we die we only become the foam on the surface of the water. Human beings, unlike us, have a soul which lives forever. It rises up through the clear, pure air beyond the glittering stars."

"Why do we not have a soul?" asked the little mermaid sadly; "I would give gladly all the hundreds of years that I have to live, to be a human being only for one day."

"You must not think of that," said the old woman; "we are much happier and much better off than human beings."

"Is there anything I can do to win an immortal soul?" asked the mermaid.

"No," said the old woman, "unless a man were to love you and he promised to be true to you here and hereafter. But this can never happen. Your fish's tail, which here we consider so beautiful, is thought on earth to be quite ugly. They do not know any better, and think it necessary to have two stout props, which they call legs, in order to be handsome."

Then the little mermaid sighed, and looked sorrowfully at her fish's tail.

"Let us be happy," said the old lady, "and dance away the three hundred years that we have to live, which is really quite long enough; after that we can rest ourselves all the better. Now, this very evening we are going to have a court ball."

The walls and the ceiling of the large ball-room were of transparent crystal. There danced the mermen and the mermaids to the music of their own sweet singing, and the little mermaid sang more sweetly than any of them. The whole court applauded her and for a moment her heart felt joyful for she knew she had the loveliest voice of all, whether on earth or in the sea. But soon she thought again of the world above, for she could not forget the charming prince, nor her sorrow that she had not an immortal soul like his.

Then she thought: "I will venture all for him, and to win an immortal soul. I will go to the sea witch, of whom I have always been so much afraid, but she can give me counsel and help."

And the little mermaid left her sisters dancing in the palace and swam to the foaming whirlpools beyond which the sorceress lived. Her house stood in the centre of a strange forest, where the trees and flowers were half animals and half plants. Each plant held in its grasp something it had seized: white skeletons of human beings who had perished at sea, oars, rudders, and chests of ships were lying tightly grasped by their clinging arms. The little mermaid's heart beat with fear, and she very nearly turned back; but she thought of the prince, and of the human soul for which she longed, and her courage returned.

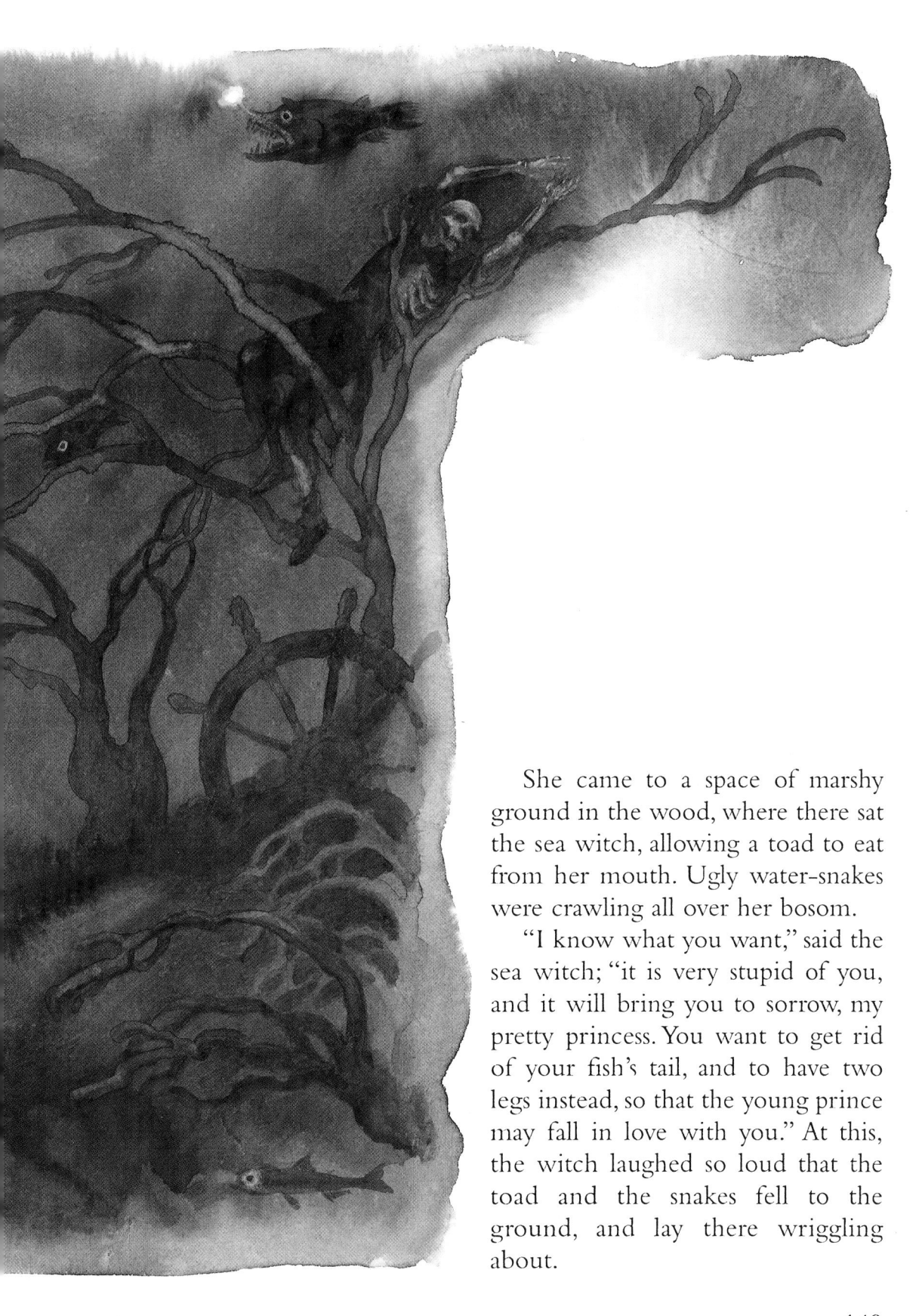

She came to a space of marshy ground in the wood, where there sat the sea witch, allowing a toad to eat from her mouth. Ugly water-snakes were crawling all over her bosom.

"I know what you want," said the sea witch; "it is very stupid of you, and it will bring you to sorrow, my pretty princess. You want to get rid of your fish's tail, and to have two legs instead, so that the young prince may fall in love with you." At this, the witch laughed so loud that the toad and the snakes fell to the ground, and lay there wriggling about.

"You will have your wish," she declared. "You must swim to land tomorrow before sunrise, and sit down on the shore and drink the potion I will prepare for you,. Your tail will disappear, and shrink up into legs. You will still have the same graceful movement, and no dancer will ever tread so lightly; but every step you take will feel like treading upon sharp knives.

"But," she continued, "once you become like a human being, you can no more be a mermaid. You will never return to your father's palace and, if you do not win the love of the prince and become man and wife, you will never have a soul. And should he marry another, your heart will break, and you will be no more than foam on the crest of the waves."

"Yet I will do it," said the little mermaid, and she became pale as death.

"But I must be paid also," said the witch, "and my price is not a trifle. You have the sweetest voice of any creature but your voice you must give to me."

"But if you take away my voice," said the little mermaid, "what is left for me?"

"Your beauty, your graceful walk, and your eyes. Surely with these you can charm a man's heart. Well, have you lost your courage? Put out your little tongue that I may cut it off, then you shall have the potion."

Then the witch placed her cauldron on the fire, and when the potion was ready, it looked like the clearest water. Then she cut off the mermaid's tongue, so that she would never again speak or sing.

The little mermaid took the magic potion and, leaving her, passed quickly through the wood, and arrived again at the rushing whirlpools. She found her father's palace dark and silent, and all within asleep; and now she was to leave them forever, she felt as if her heart would break. She kissed her hand a thousand times towards the palace, and then rose up through the dark blue waters.

When she came in sight of the prince's palace, the little mermaid drank the magic draught, and it seemed as if a two-edged sword went through her delicate body. She fainted and lay like one dead.

When the sun arose and shone over the sea, she awoke and felt a sharp pain; but just before her stood the handsome young prince. He fixed his eyes upon her so earnestly that she cast down her gaze, and then became aware that her fish's tail was gone, and that she had a pretty pair of white legs and tiny feet, but she had no clothes, so she wrapped herself in her long, thick hair.

The prince asked her who she was, and where she came from, and she looked at him with her deep blue eyes; but she could not speak. He put out his hand and she followed. Every step she took was like treading upon needles or sharp knives; but she bore it willingly, and stepped as lightly by the prince's side towards the palace stairs. She was very soon dressed in robes of silk and muslin, and was the most lovely creature in the place; but she was dumb, and could neither speak nor sing.

Then the musicians began to play fairy-like dances, and the little mermaid raised her lovely arms, stood on the tips of her toes, and danced as no one there had ever seen. Every one was enchanted, especially the prince, and she danced again quite readily to please him, though each time her foot touched the floor it seemed as if she trod on sharp knives.

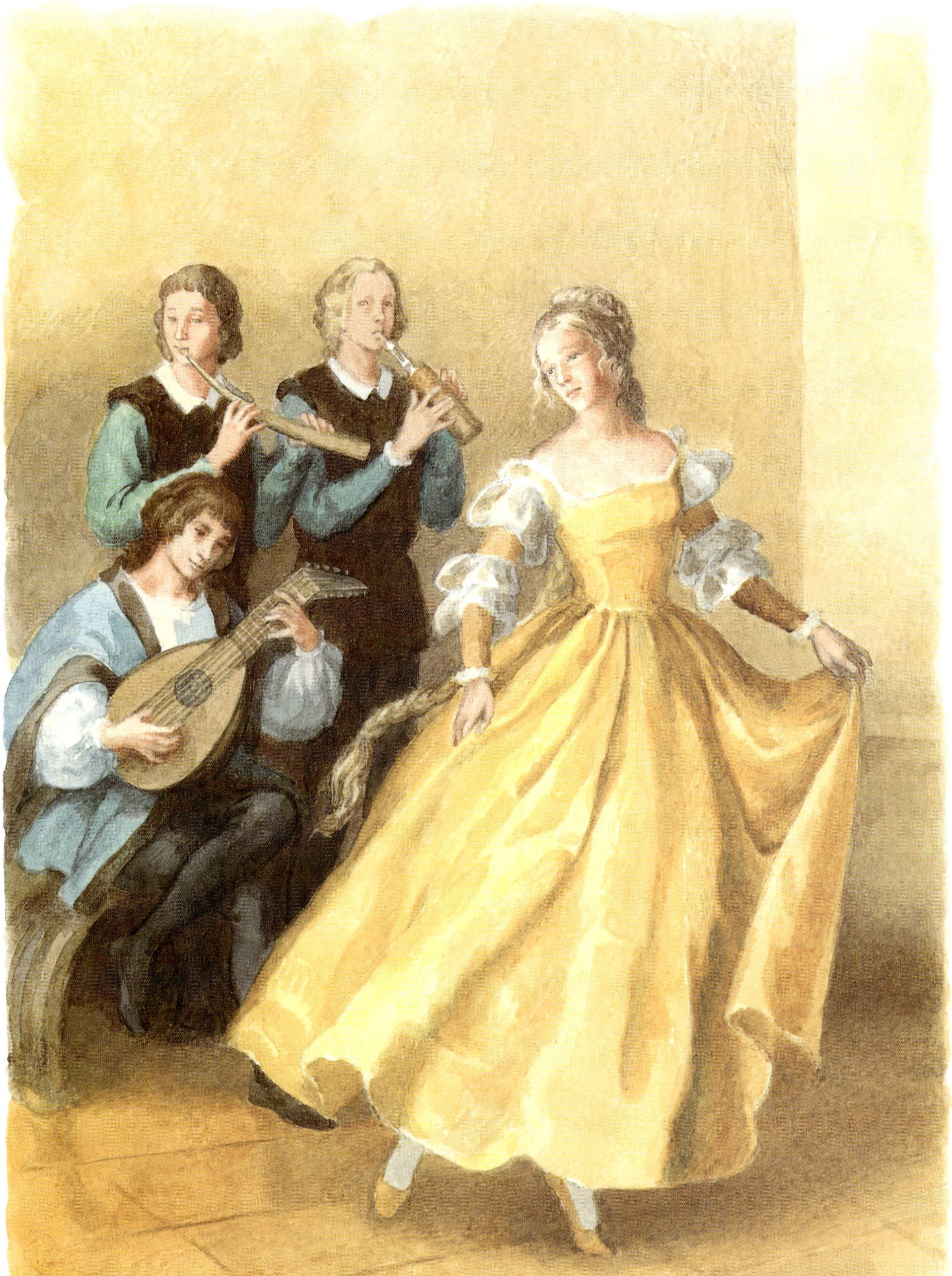

The prince said she should remain with him always, and from that day on she slept at his door on a velvet cushion. When all were asleep, she would go and sit on the broad marble steps and think of those below in the deep sea.

Once her sisters came up, singing sorrowfully as they floated on the water. She called out to them, and they told her how much her going had saddened them. After that, they came every night.

As the days passed, she loved the prince more fondly, and though he loved her as a little child, he never thought to make her his wife.

"Do you not love me?" her eyes seemed to say, when he took her in his arms and kissed her fair forehead.

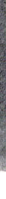

"Yes, you are dear to me," said the prince; "for you are like a young maiden whom I once saw, but whom I shall never meet again. I was in a ship that was wrecked, and the waves cast me ashore near a holy temple. The youngest of the temple maidens found me and saved my life. She is the only one in the world whom I could love, but she belongs to the holy temple. You are like her, and my good fortune has sent you to me instead of her; and we will never part."

"Ah, he knows not that it was I who saved his life," thought the little mermaid. "I saw the pretty maiden that he loves better than he loves me;" and the mermaid sighed deeply, but she could not shed tears. "They will meet no more but I am by his side, and see him every day. I will take care of him, and love him, and give up my life for his sake."

Very soon it was announced that the prince must marry the beautiful daughter of a neighbouring king. A fine ship was being fitted out for the journey and a great company were to go with him.

"I must see this beautiful princess," said he, as they stood on the deck of the noble ship carrying them to the neighbouring country. "My parents desire it; but I cannot love her; she is not like the beautiful maiden in the temple, whom you resemble. If I were forced to choose a bride, I would rather choose you, my silent foundling, with those lovely eyes." And then he kissed her rosy mouth and laid his head on her heart, while she dreamed of human happiness and of an immortal soul.

The next morning the ship sailed into a beautiful harbour. The church bells were ringing, and from the high towers sounded a flourish of trumpets; but the princess had not yet appeared.

At last she came, and the little mermaid thought she had never seen a more perfect vision of beauty. Her skin was delicately fair, and beneath her long dark eye-lashes her laughing blue eyes shone with truth and purity.

"It was you," cried the prince, "who saved my life when I lay dead on the beach," and he folded the blushing princess in his arms. "Oh, I am too happy," said he. "My fondest hopes are all fulfilled."

But the little mermaid felt as if her heart were already broken. His wedding morning would bring death to her, and she would change into the foam of the sea.

All the church bells rung, and the heralds rode about the town proclaiming the betrothal, and soon afterwards the bishop blessed their marriage. That evening the bride and bridegroom went on board ship where a costly tent of purple and gold had been erected and the ship, with swelling sails and a favourable wind, glided away over the calm sea.

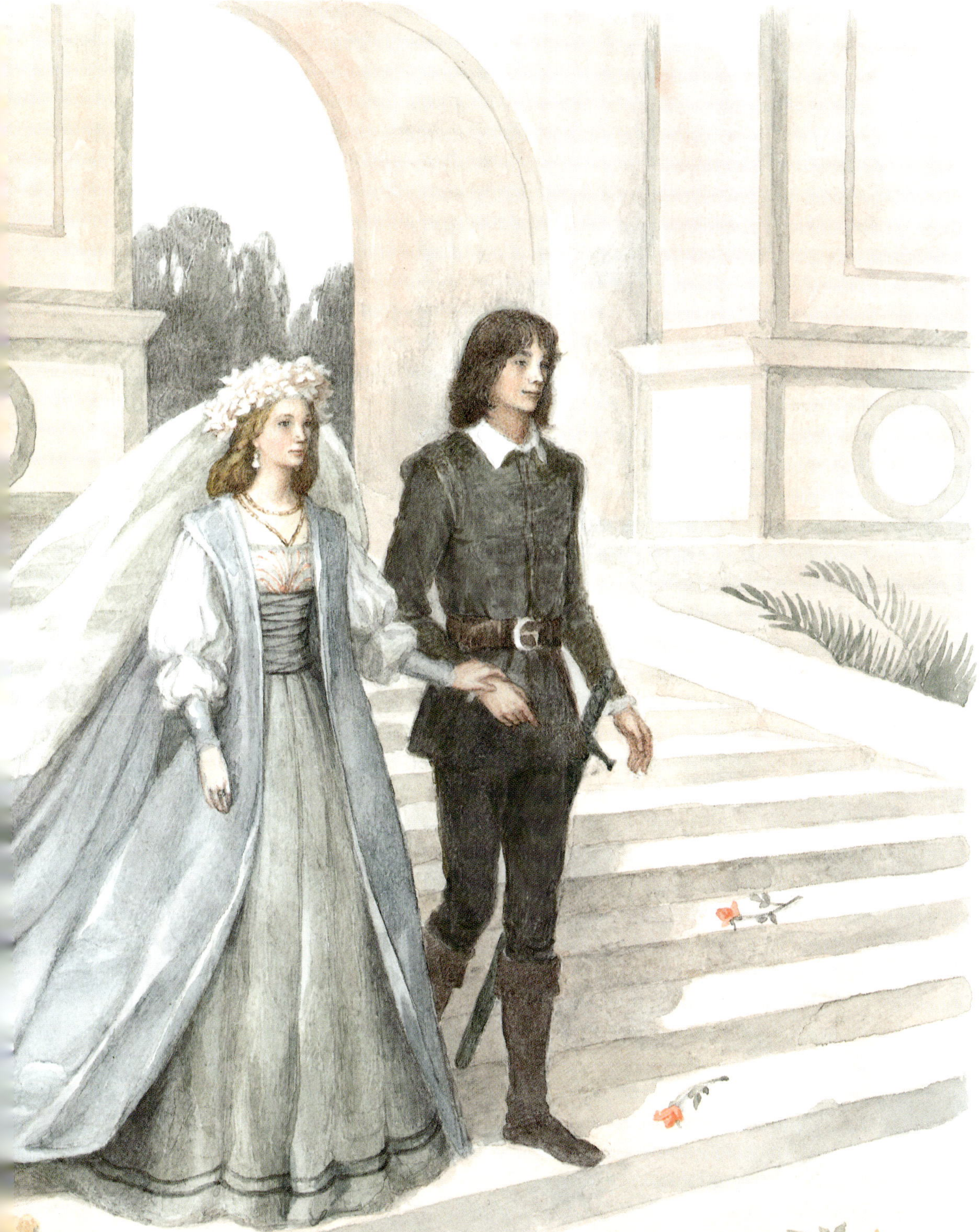

All was joy and gaiety on board ship till long after midnight; she laughed and danced with the rest, while thoughts of death were in her heart. The prince kissed his beautiful bride till they went arm-in-arm to rest in the splendid tent. Then all became still on board the ship. The little mermaid leaned her white arms on the edge of the vessel, and looked towards the east for the first ray of dawn that would bring her death. She saw her sisters rising out of the flood: they were as pale as herself; but their long beautiful hair waved no more in the wind, and had been cut off.

"We have given our hair to the witch," said they, "to obtain help for you, that you may not die to-night. She has given us a knife: here it is, see it is very sharp. Before the sun rises you must plunge it into the heart of the prince; when the warm blood falls upon your feet they will form into a fish's tail, and you will be once more a mermaid, and return to us to live out your three hundred years. Hurry, for he or you must die before sunrise."

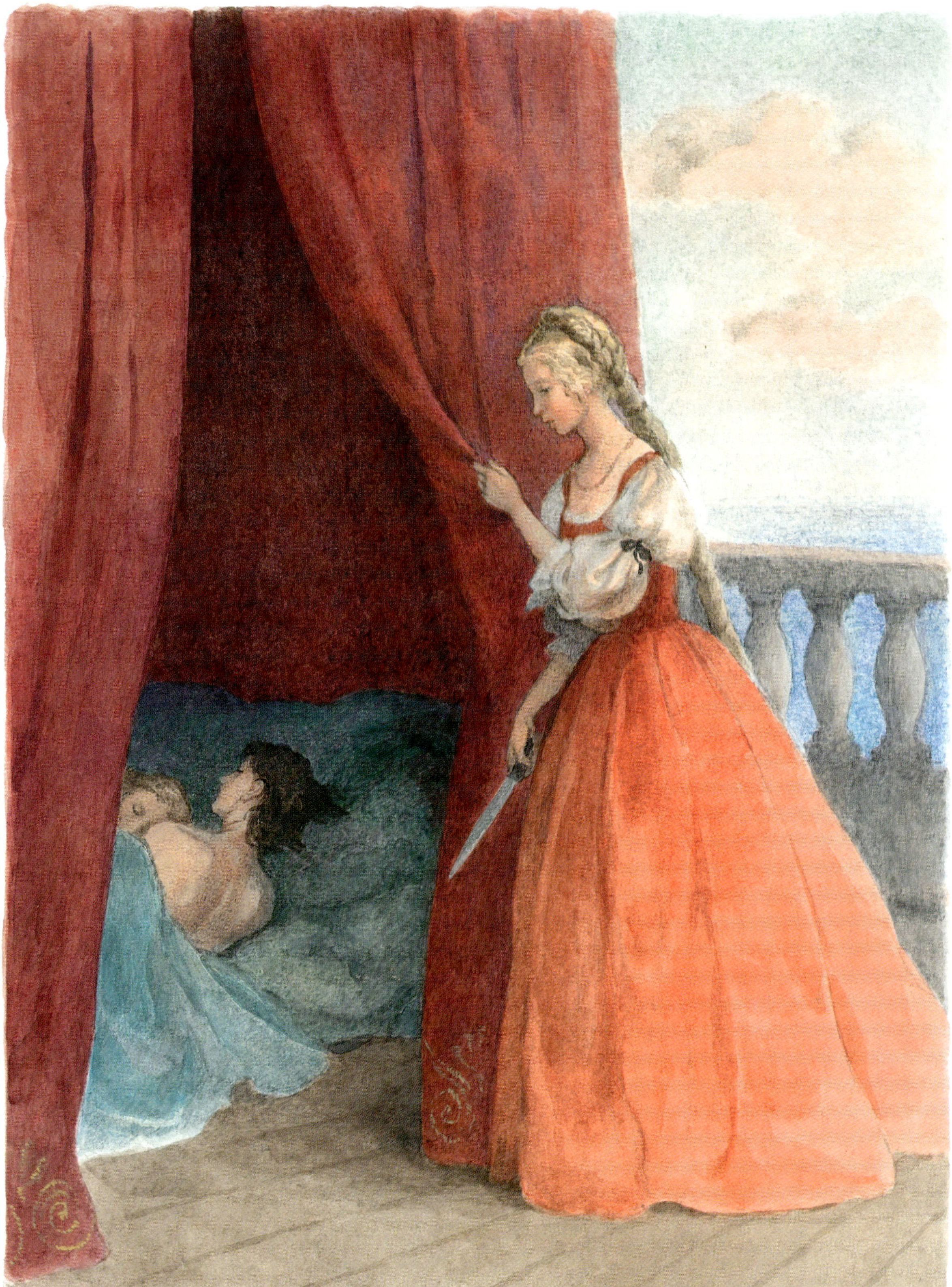

The little mermaid drew back the crimson curtain of the tent, and beheld the fair bride with her head resting on the prince's breast. She bent down and kissed his fair brow, then looked at the sky on which the rosy dawn grew brighter and brighter; then she glanced at the sharp knife, and again fixed her eyes on the prince, who whispered the name of his bride in his dreams. She was in his thoughts, and the knife trembled in the hand of the little mermaid: then she flung it far away from her into the waves.

She cast one more lingering, half-fainting glance at the prince, and then threw herself from the ship into the sea, and thought her body was dissolving into foam. The sun rose above the waves, and its warm rays fell on the little mermaid, who did not feel as if she were dying. Suddenly all around her floated hundreds of transparent beautiful beings. The little mermaid saw that she had a body like theirs, and that she continued to rise higher and higher out of the foam. "Where am I?" asked she, and her voice sounded heavenly, like the voices of those around her; unlike any earthly music.

"You are among the daughters of the air," answered one of them. "A mermaid has not an immortal soul, nor can she obtain one unless she wins the love of a human being. But the daughters of the air, although they do not possess an immortal soul, can earn themselves a soul by their good deeds. You, poor little mermaid, have tried with your whole heart to do as we are doing; you have suffered and endured and raised yourself to the spirit-world by your good deeds; and now, by striving for three hundred years in the same way, you may obtain an immortal soul."

The little mermaid lifted her eyes towards the sun, and felt them, for the first time, filling with tears. On the ship, where she had left the prince, there were life and noise; she saw him and his beautiful bride searching for her. Sorrowfully they gazed at the pearly foam, as if they knew she had thrown herself into the waves. Unseen she kissed the bride's forehead and fanned the cheek of the prince, and then mounted with the other children of the air to a rosy cloud that floated through the ether.

"After three hundred years, so shall we float into the kingdom of heaven," said one of the children of the air.

"And we may even get there sooner," whispered one of her companions, "for every time we find a good child, our waiting is shortened. When we fly through the house, we smile with joy, because for each good child we can count one year less of our three hundred years. When we see a naughty child, though, we shed tears of sorrow, and for every tear a day is added to our time of trial!"

The Fir Tree

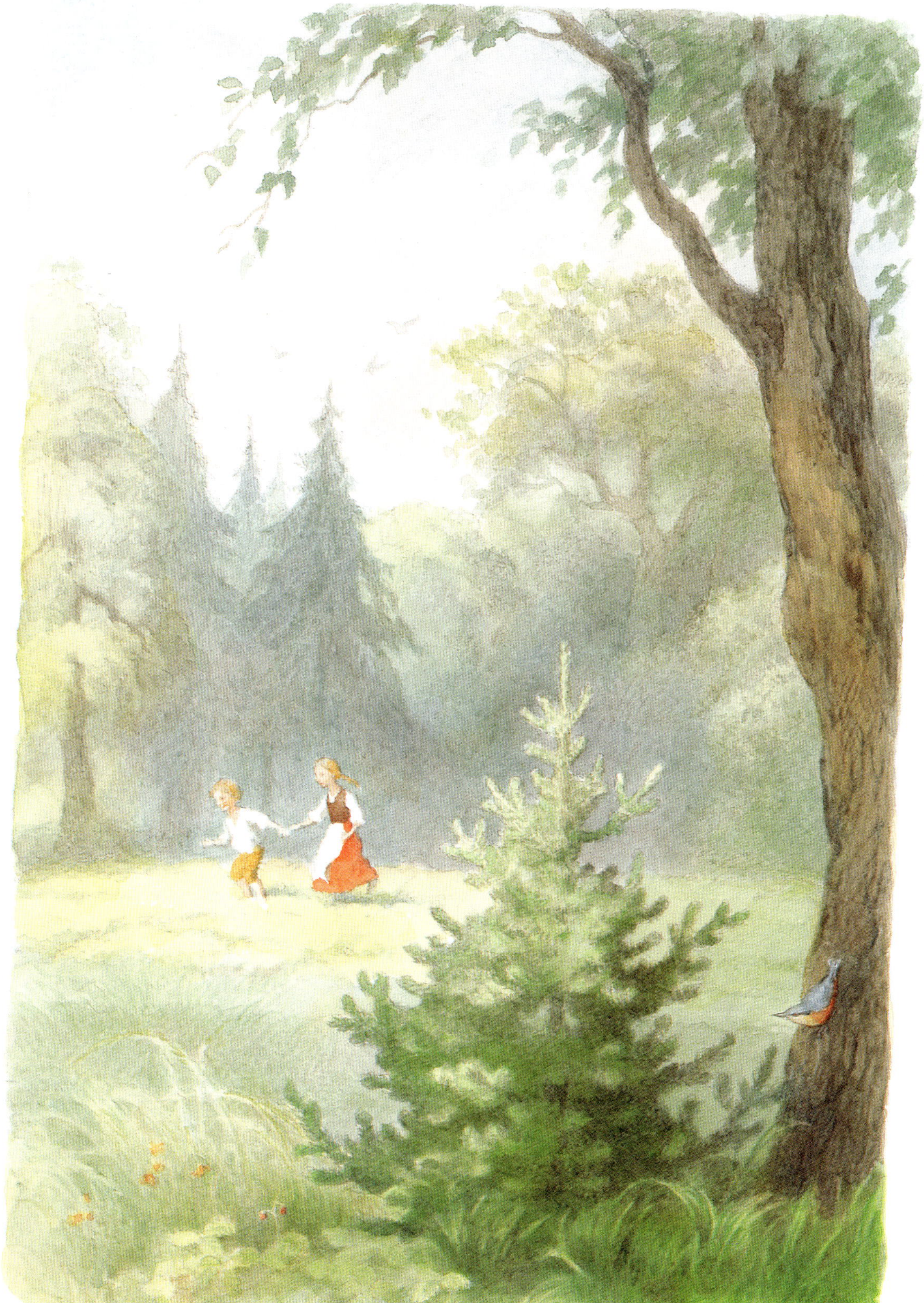

FAR down in the forest, there grew a pretty little fir-tree; and yet it was not happy, it wished so much to be tall like its companions — the pines and firs which grew around it. The sun shone, and the soft air fluttered its leaves, and the little children passed by, prattling merrily, but the fir-tree took no heed of them.

As it grew, it still complained, "Oh! how I wish I were as tall as the other trees, then I would spread out my branches and my top would overlook the wide world. I should have the birds building their nests on my boughs, and when the wind blew, I should bow with stately dignity like my tall companions."

The tree was so discontented, that it took no pleasure in the warm sunshine, the birds, or the rosy clouds that floated over it morning and evening.

Two winters passed, and the tree had grown really tall. Yet it remained unsatisfied. In the autumn, as usual, the wood-cutters came and cut down several of the tallest trees, and the young fir-tree shuddered as the noble trees fell to the earth with a crash. Then they were drawn by horses out of the forest. "Where were they going? What would become of them?" The young fir-tree wished to understand; so in the spring, it asked the swallows and the stork what they knew of that.

The swallows knew nothing, but the stork nodded his head, and said, "Yes, I think I know what became of them. I saw several new ships as I flew from Egypt, and they had fine masts that smelt like fir. Those must have been the trees; they were very stately."

"Oh, how I wish I were tall enough to go on the sea," said the fir-tree.

"Rejoice in your youth," said the sunbeam; "rejoice in your fresh growth, and the young life that is in you." But the fir-tree paid no regard.

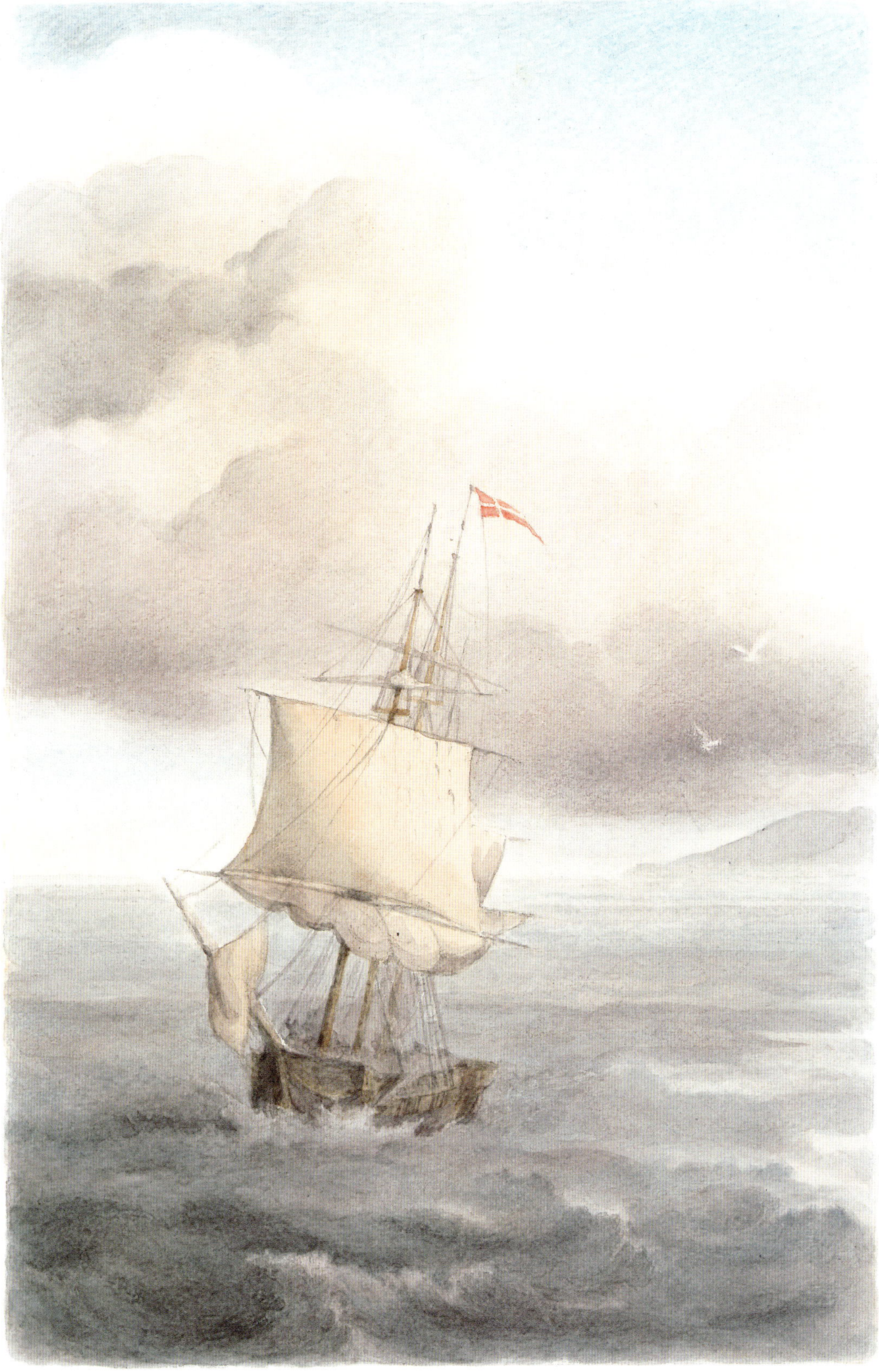

Christmas-time drew near, and many young trees were cut down, some smaller and younger than the fir-tree. These young trees kept their branches, and were laid on wagons and drawn out of the forest.

"Where are they going?" asked the fir-tree.

"We know, we know," sang the sparrows. "We see them through the windows of the houses in town, dressed up in the most splendid way. They stand in the middle of a room, decorated with all sorts of pretty things — cakes, gilded apples, toys, and lots of candles."

"Will anything so brilliant ever happen to me?" thought the fir-tree. "Oh! when will Christmas be here?"

"Rejoice with us," said the air and the sunlight. "Enjoy your own bright life in the fresh air."

But the tree would not rejoice, though it grew taller every day, and passers-by started to say, "What a beautiful tree!"

A short time before Christmas, the discontented fir-tree was the first to fall. As the tree toppled with a groan to the earth, it knew that it should never again see the forest or the little bushes and many-coloured flowers that had grown by its side, perhaps not even the birds.

Neither was the journey at all pleasant. The tree recovered while being unpacked in the courtyard of a house, to hear a man say, "We only want one, and this is the prettiest."

Then came two servants and carried the fir-tree to the house and into a large and beautiful room.

On the walls hung pictures, and there were rocking chairs, silken sofas, large tables, covered with pictures, books, and so many toys. The fir-tree was placed in a large tub, full of sand; but green baize hung all around it, and it stood on a very handsome carpet. How the fir-tree trembled! "What was going to happen to him now?"

Some young ladies came, and the servants helped them to decorate the tree. On one branch they hung little bags cut out of coloured paper, and each bag was filled with sweets. From other branches hung gilded apples and walnuts, as if they had grown there; and above, and all round, were lots of red, blue, and white candles. Tiny dolls were placed under the green needles — the tree had never seen such things before — and at the very top was fastened a glittering star, made of tinsel. Oh, it was very beautiful!

"This evening," they all exclaimed, "when the candles are lit, how bright it will be!"

"Oh, that the evening were come," thought the tree, "and the candles lit!"

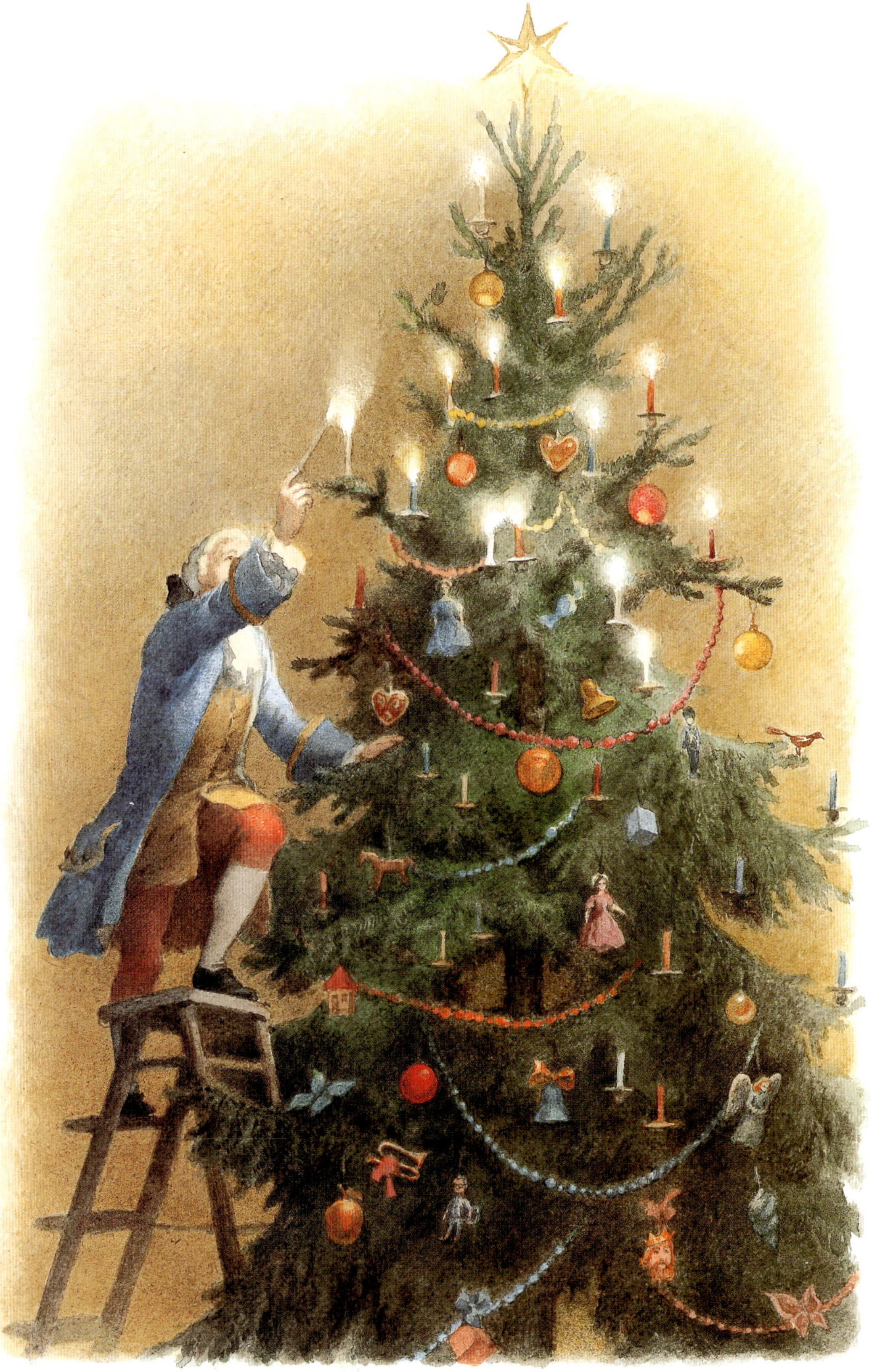

At last the moment came for the candles to be lit, and then what a blaze of light the tree presented! It trembled so with joy in all its branches, that one of the candles fell among the green needles and burnt some of them. "Help!" exclaimed the young ladies, but there was no danger, for they quickly extinguished the fire. After this, the tree tried not to tremble at all, though the fire frightened him.

And now the folding doors were thrown open, and a troop of children rushed in, followed more silently by their elders. For a moment the little ones stood silent, then they shouted for joy and danced merrily round the tree, while one present after another was taken from it.

"What are they doing? What will happen next?" thought the fir. At last the candles burnt down and were put out. Then the children received permission to plunder the tree.

Oh, how they rushed upon it, till the branches cracked, and had it not been fastened to the ceiling, it would have been thrown down. The children then danced about with their pretty toys, and no one noticed the tree, except the children's maid who came and peeped among the branches to see if an apple or a fig had been forgotten.

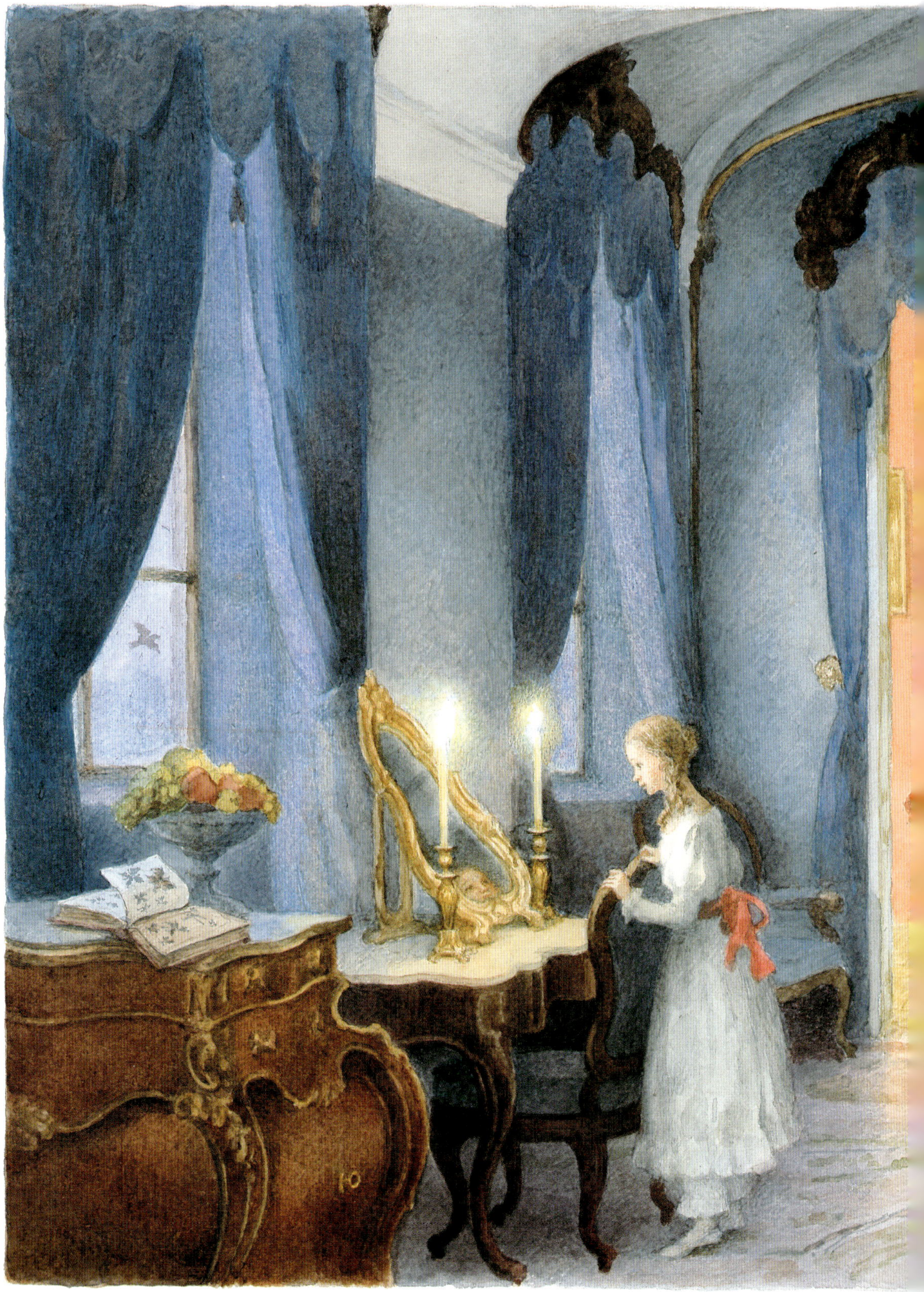

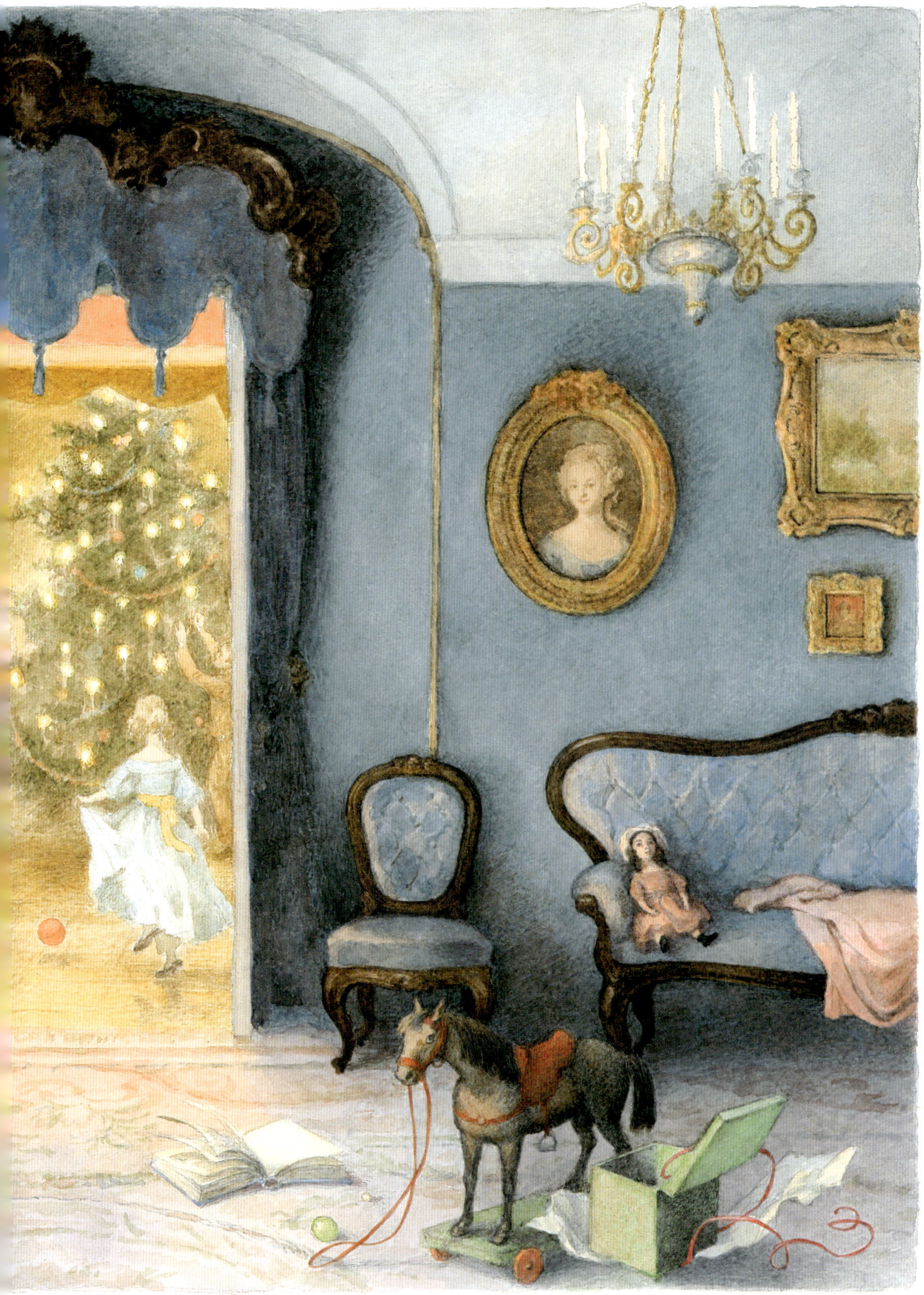

"A story, a story," cried the children, pulling a little fat man towards the tree.

"Here we shall be in the shade," said the man, as he seated himself under it, "and the tree will have the pleasure of hearing also, but I shall only tell one story. What shall it be? Chicken-Licken? Or Humpty Dumpty, who fell downstairs, but soon got up again, and in the end married a princess."

"Chicken-Licken," cried some. "Humpty Dumpty," cried others, and there was much shouting. Then the old man told them the story of Humpty Dumpty, how he fell downstairs, and was raised up again, and married a princess. After this the fir-tree became quite silent and thoughtful. Never had the birds in the forest told such a tale as "Humpty Dumpty."

"So this is how it is in the world," thought the fir-tree; he believed it all, because it was told by such a nice man. "Ah! well," he thought, "who knows? perhaps I may fall down too, and marry a princess;" and he looked forward joyfully to the next evening, expecting the same pleasures again.

"Tomorrow," thought he, "I will enjoy the same splendour, and perhaps I shall hear the story of Humpty Dumpty again."

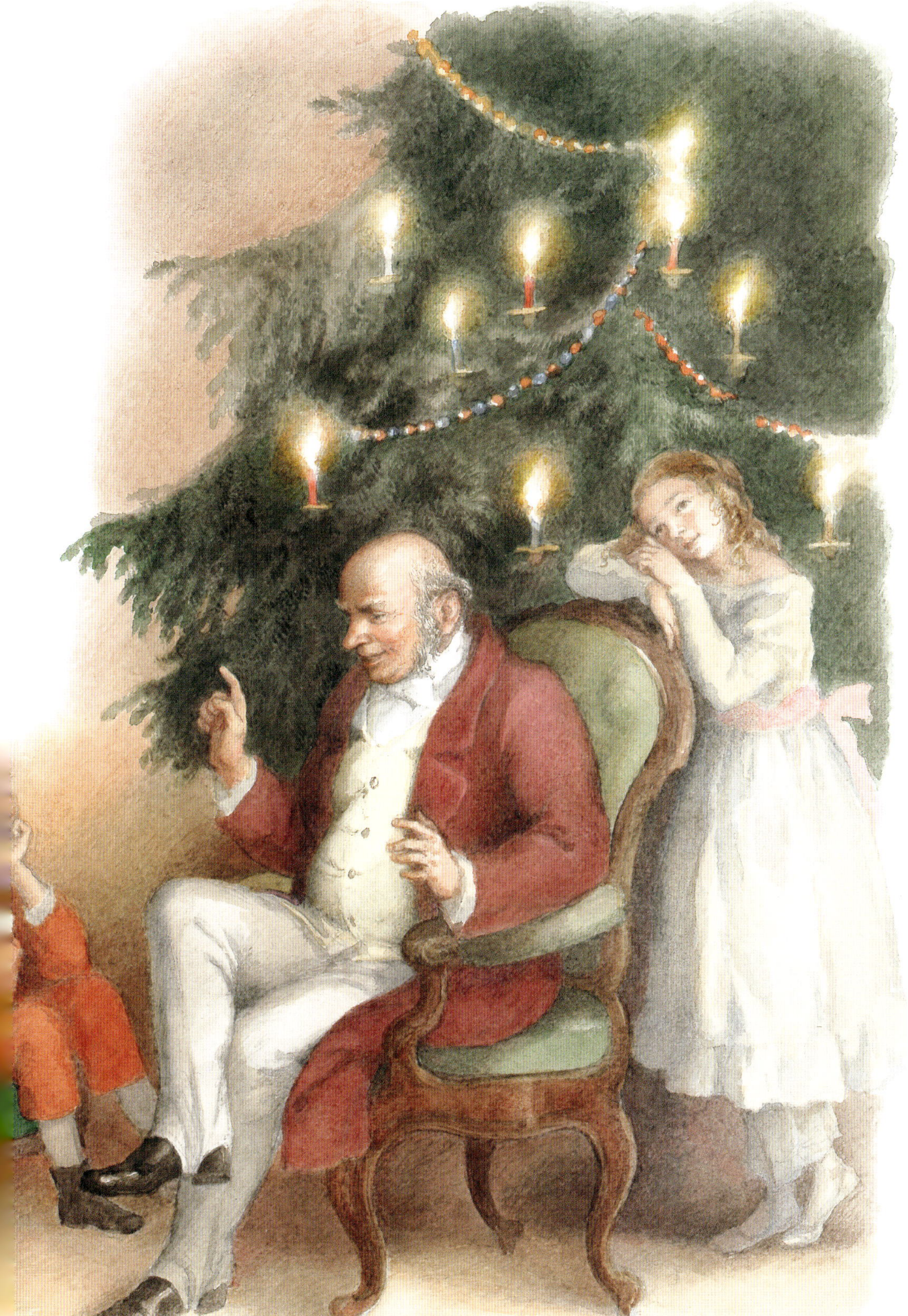

In the morning the servants and the housemaid came in.

"Now," thought the fir, "I am to be dressed in glittering candles again." But they dragged him out of the room and upstairs to the attic, and threw him in a dark corner, and there they left him.

"What does this mean?" thought the tree, "what am I to do here?" And he had time enough to think, for days and nights passed and no one came near him.

"It is winter now," thought the tree, "I shall be sheltered here, I dare say, until spring comes and I am taken out to be planted. How thoughtful and kind everybody is to me! Still I wish this place were not so dark, as well as lonely. How pleasant it was out in the forest while the snow lay on the ground, when the children would run by. Oh! it is so lonely here."

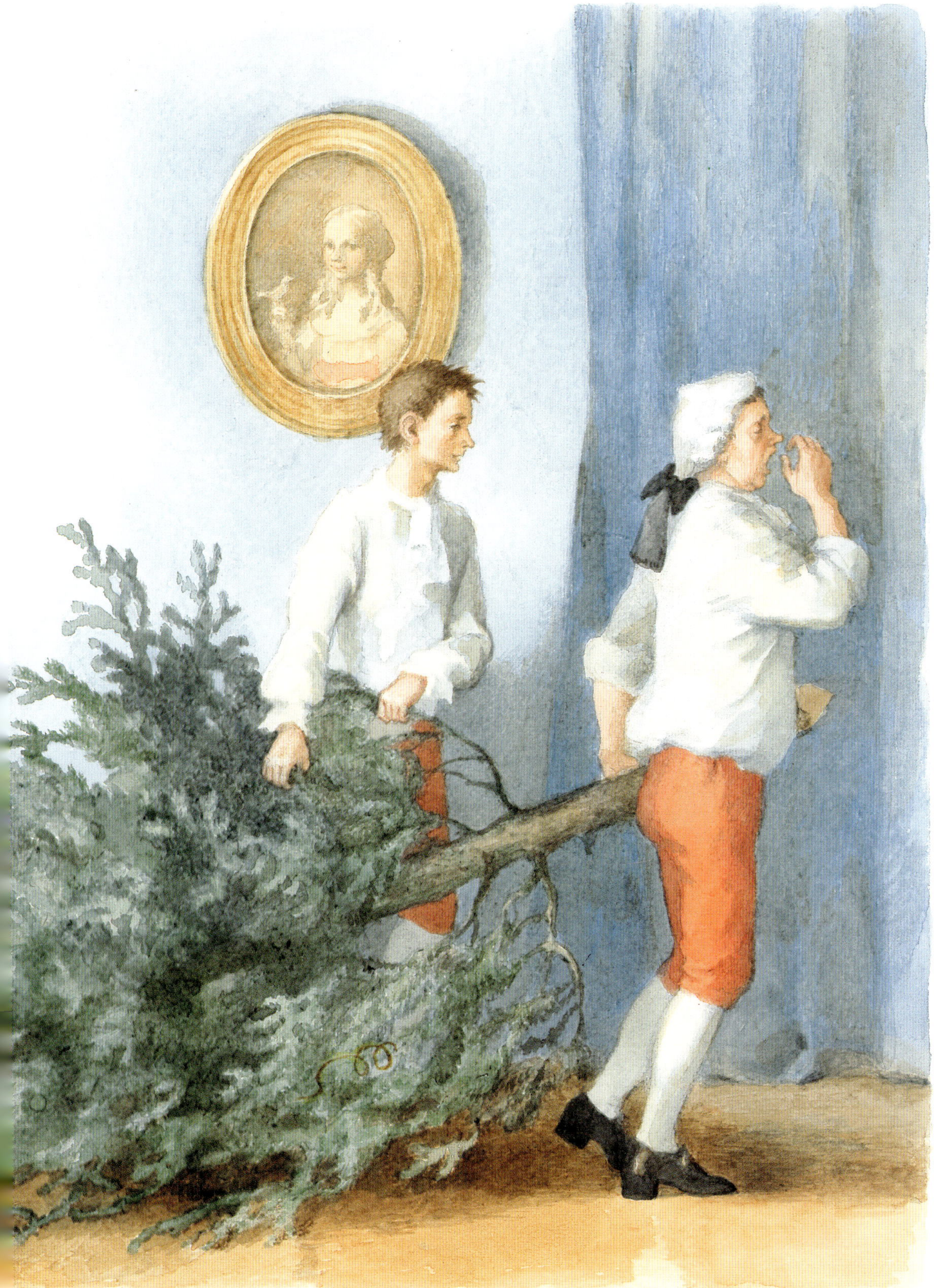

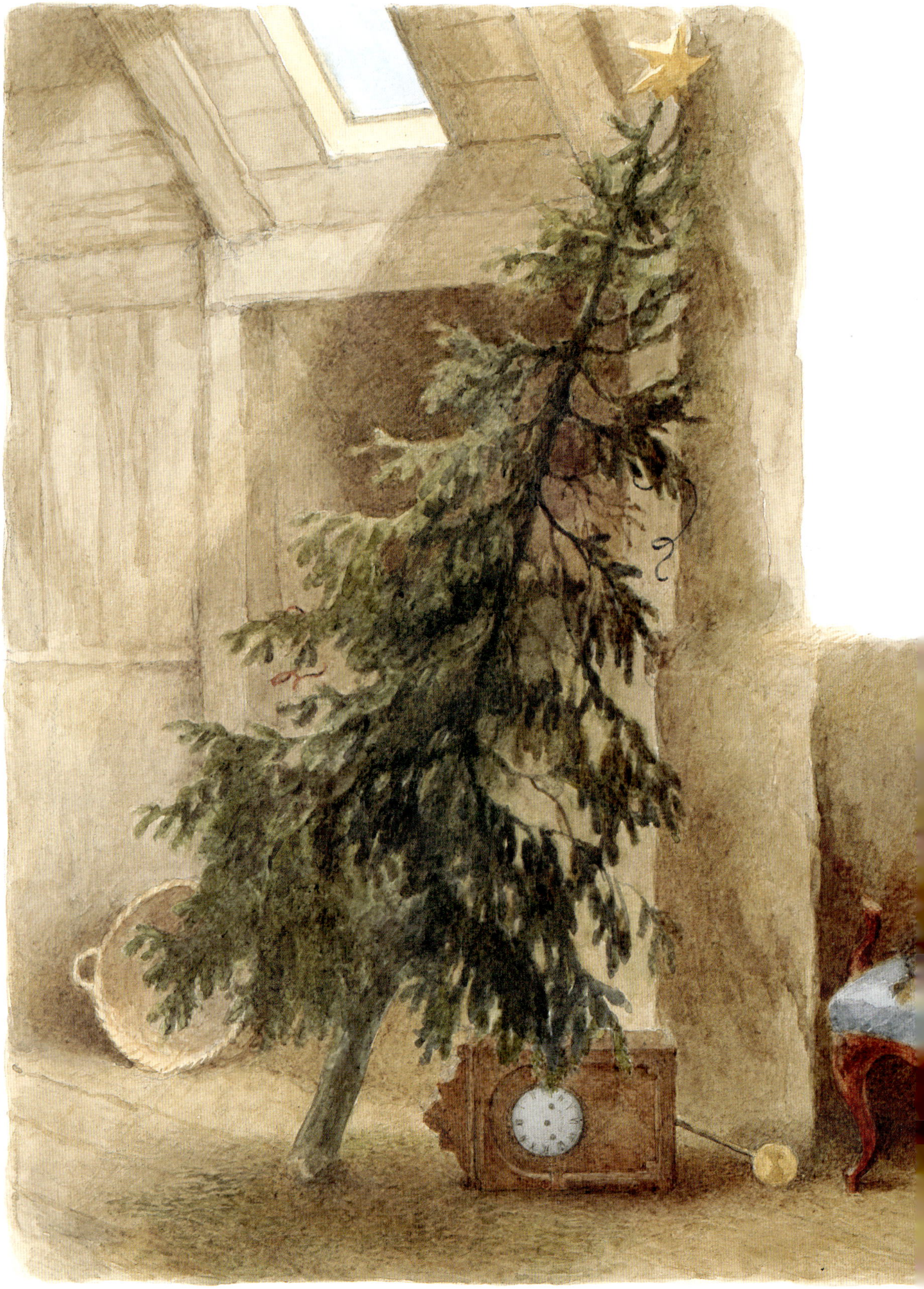

"Squeak, squeak," said a little mouse, creeping towards the tree; then came another; and they both sniffed at the fir-tree and crept between the branches.

"Oh, it is very cold," said the little mouse, "or else we should be so comfortable here, shouldn't we, you old fir-tree?"

"I am not old," said the fir-tree, "there are many older than I am."

"Where do you come from? and what do you know?" asked the mice, who were full of curiosity. "Have you seen the most beautiful places in the world, and can you tell us all about them? and have you been in the storeroom, where cheeses lie on the shelf, and hams hang from the ceiling?"

"I know nothing of that place," said the fir-tree, "but I know the wood where the sun shines and the birds sing." And then the tree told the little mice all about its youth. They had never heard such stories in their lives; and after they had listened, they said, "What wonderful things you have seen! You must have been very happy."

"Happy!" exclaimed the fir-tree, and then as he reflected further, he said, "Ah, yes! after all those were happy days." When he went on and told them how he had been dressed up with cakes and lights, the mice said again, "How happy you must have been!"

The next night, four other mice came with them to hear the tree's memories. The more he talked the more he remembered, and then he thought to himself, "Those were happy days, but they may come again. Humpty Dumpty fell down stairs, and he married the princess; perhaps I may marry a princess too."

"Who is Humpty Dumpty?" asked the little mice. And the tree told the whole story; he could remember every single word, and the little mice was so delighted with it, that they were ready to jump to the top of the tree. The next night a great many more mice made their appearance, and on Sunday two rats came with them; but they said, it was not a nice story at all, and the little mice were very sorry, for it made them also think less of it.

"Do you know only one story?" asked the rats.

"Only one," replied the fir-tree; "I heard it on the happiest evening of my life; but I did not know I was so happy at the time."

"We think it is a very miserable story," said the rats. "Don't you know any story about bacon?"

"No," replied the tree.

"Many thanks to you then," replied the rats, and they marched off.

The little mice also kept away after this, and the tree sighed, and said, "It was very pleasant when the little mice sat around and listened to me. Now that is all past. I shall think myself happy when someone comes to take me out of here."

One morning people came to clear out the garret, and the tree was pulled out of the corner, then the servant dragged it out upon the staircase where the daylight shone.

"Now life is beginning again," said the tree, rejoicing in the sunshine and fresh air. It was carried down stairs and taken into the courtyard close to a garden, where everything looked blooming. Fresh and fragrant roses hung over the little palings. The linden-trees were in blossom; while the swallows flew here and there, singing.

"Now I shall live," cried the tree, joyfully spreading out its branches; but alas! they were all withered and yellow. Yet the star of gold paper still stuck in the top of the tree and glittered in the sunshine.

Two of the same children were playing there who had danced round the tree at Christmas. The youngest saw the gilded star, and ran and pulled it off the tree.

"Look what's here on the withered old fir-tree," said the child, treading on the branches till they crackled under his boots. And the tree saw all the fresh bright flowers in the garden, and then looked at itself, lying in the weeds and nettles. It thought of its fresh youth in the forest, of the merry Christmas evening, and of the little mice who had listened to the story of "Humpty Dumpty."

"All past!" said the old tree; "Oh, if only I'd enjoyed myself while I had the chance! But now it is too late."

Then a lad came and chopped the tree into small pieces, which he threw in a fire and as they quickly blazed up, the tree sighed so deeply that each sigh was like a pistol-shot. The children who were at play, came and seated themselves in front of the fire, and the youngest still held in his hand the golden star, which the tree had worn during the happiest evening of its life.

Now all was past; the tree's life and the story, too — for all stories must come to an end at last.

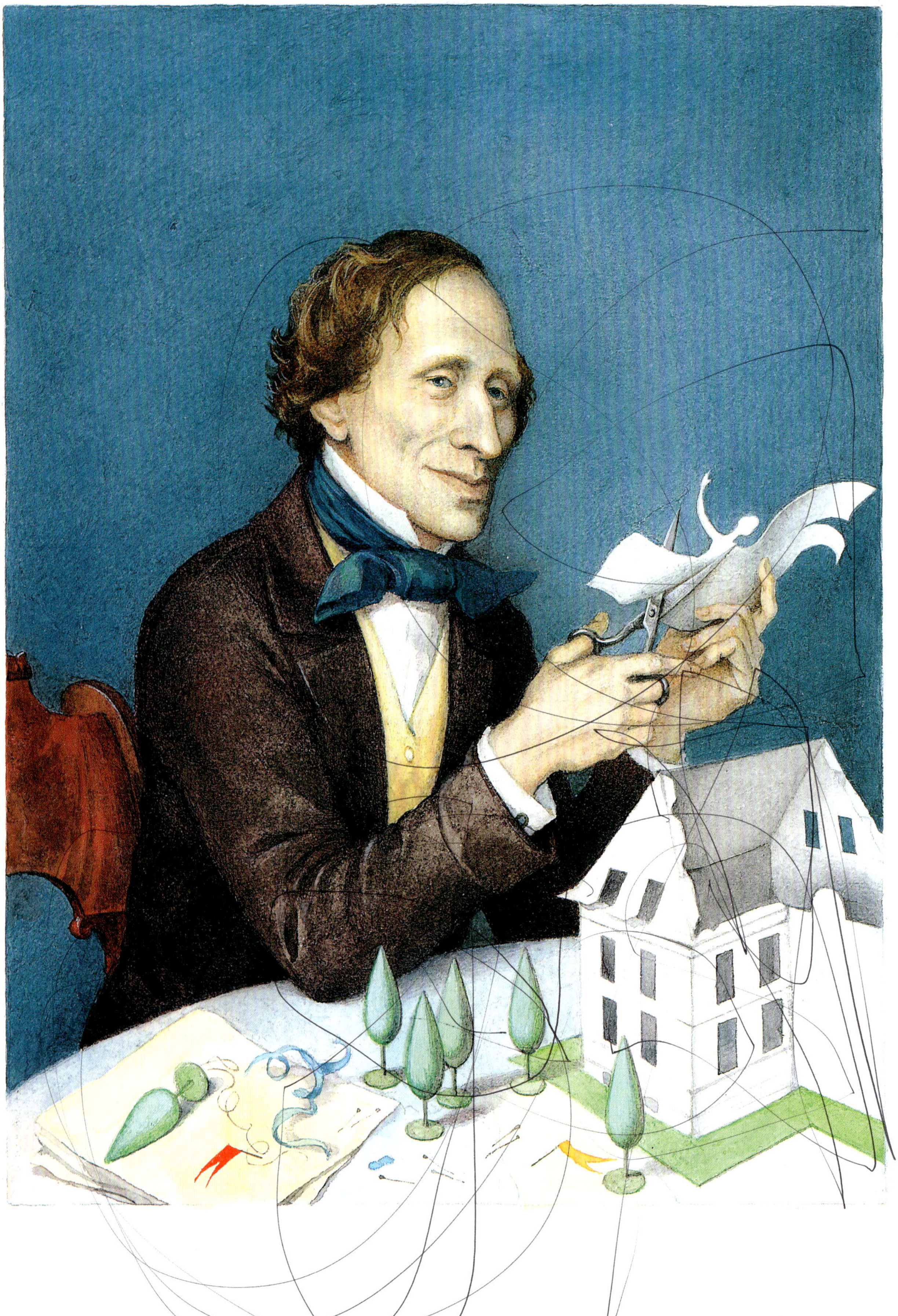

The Storyteller
Hans Christian Andersen

IN THE city of Odense, in Denmark, there lived a poor shoemaker and his wife in a tiny house. They were simple folk and the shoemaker's wife could barely read or write. They had a son called Hans Christian whom the father doted on and with whom he spent his time playing and reading aloud. Together they made toys and paper cut-outs, and created model theatre shows, using puppets which they made out of simple materials.

Later in life, Hans Christian wrote about the tiny house he lived in: "One small room that was almost taken up by the shoemaker's bench, the bed and the settle where I used to sleep, was my childhood home. But the walls were hung with pictures; pretty cups, glasses and ornaments stood on the chest of drawers... From the kitchen, with the help of a ladder you got on to the roof where, in the gutter between our house and the neighbour's, was... my mother's entire garden. It still flourishes in my fairy tale *The Snow Queen.*"

The father who laughed and played with the boy and did so much to bring his imagination to life, died when Hans Christian was only eleven years old, and his mother was forced to take on work as a washerwoman.

From these simple beginnings, Hans Christian grew up to be Denmark's most famous storyteller whose tales have been translated and told all around the world. Like the memory of his mother's little roof garden, many similar details of his childhood are found in his stories. *The Ugly Duckling,* which tells of an ungainly and despised chick who grows up to be a handsome swan, admired by all, is the tale he spun around his own life.

Hans Christian Andersen was born in 1805 and died in 1875. In his long lifetime, he wrote poetry, plays, novels and books about his travels around Europe. But it was his one hundred and fifty *Fairy Tales and Stories* that took the art of storytelling into a new realm of bittersweet fantasy and made him famous as a writer.